P9-BYT-349

ACCLAIM FOR THE NOVELS OF OPAL CAREW

"Opal Carew is a genius at spinning the most erotic stories by tapping into forbidden fantasies and visiting emotions that bring the characters literally to their knees. A steamy-hot read!"

—*Fresh Fiction* on *Pleasure Bound*

"Carew's book reminds me of a really good box of chocolates that you want to savor, but can't help eating all up in one sitting because it's so decadent and yummy. Feast on this one today!"

—*Night Owl Romance* on *Bliss*

"A blazing hot erotic romp . . . a must-read for lovers of erotic romance. A fabulously fun and stupendously steamy read for a cold winter's night. This one's so hot, you might need to wear oven mitts while you're reading it!"

—*Romance Junkies* on *Swing*

"Carew definitely knows how to turn up the heat, and her descriptions of the physical and mental aspects of BDSM are spot on . . . this book deserves a spot on top of your to-be-read pile."

—*RT Book Reviews* on *Secret Ties*

"Opal Carew brings erotic romance to a whole new level. . . . She sets your senses on fire!"

—*Reader to Reader*

"Delicious in its sensuality. Opal Carew has a great imagination and her sensual scenes are sure to get a fire going in many readers."

—*A Romance Review*

"Opal Carew is truly a goddess of sensuality in her writing."

—*Dark Angel Reviews*

"I recommend Opal Carew for the adventuresome who don't mind singeing their senses."

—*Regency Reader*

"Carew pulls off another scorcher. . . . She knows how to write a love scene that takes her reader to dizzying heights of pleasure."

—*My Romance Story*

Illicit

ALSO BY OPAL CAREW

Bliss
Forbidden Heat
Secret Ties
Six
Blush
Swing
Twin Fantasies
Pleasure Bound
Total Abandon
Secret Weapon
Insatiable

Illicit

Opal Carew

ST. MARTIN'S GRIFFIN

NEW YORK

This is a work of fiction. All of the characters, organizations, and events portrayed in this novel are either products of the author's imagination or are used fictitiously.

ILLICIT. Copyright © 2013 by Opal Carew. All rights reserved. Printed in the United States of America. For information, address St. Martin's Press, 175 Fifth Avenue, New York, NY 10010.

www.stmartins.com

ISBN 978-0-312-67462-5 (trade paperback)
ISBN 978-1-250-01593-8 (e-book)

St. Martin's Griffin books may be purchased for educational, business, or promotional use. For information on bulk purchases, please contact Macmillan Corporate and Premium Sales Department at 1-800-221-7945 extension 5442 or write specialmarkets@macmillan.com.

First Edition: March 2013

10 9 8 7 6 5 4 3 2 1

To Laurie,
Here's to rockin' it as a team

Illicit

One

I do, too, have sexual fantasies.

Lindsay's hands clenched into fists as she strode across the lobby. Leave it to her stepmother, Audrey, to assume Lindsay's relationship with Glen had failed so miserably because Lindsay wasn't adventurous enough in the bedroom.

She couldn't bring herself to tell Audrey that the reason the relationship had ended so suddenly was because she'd walked in on the jerk in bed with two women. Anger still burned through her at the memory. It had happened weeks ago, but her discussion with Audrey over lunch had brought it all crashing back.

She sucked in a breath. Right now, all she wanted to do was get up to Jill's apartment where she could kick back over a glass of wine and rant to her best friend.

She heard a *ding* and glanced up to see the elevator doors closing ahead.

"Wait," she called and raced for the doors.

A man crossed in front of her and she weaved around him, then made a last dash for the elevator. Someone inside must have pushed the button because the doors opened again. Her high heel caught as she raced inside and she stumbled forward, landing face-first into a solid masculine chest. Hard. Rippled with smooth ridges. And naked.

"You okay?" the owner of the chest asked, as his strong hands grasped her shoulders and steadied her.

She turned around and gazed downward, nodding, her cheeks flushed.

"Yeah, sorry."

The man and his two companions—at least she assumed they were all together—wore swimsuits and had towels in hand. There was a pool on the roof of the apartment building. Maybe they'd been to the gym and had worked up a sweat and were now heading up for a swim. She immediately realized the weight room was near the pool, so that didn't make any sense, but she liked thinking about the hard-ridged muscles she'd felt when she'd fallen against Mr. X being strained and stretched while he pulled weights, his body glistening with sweat.

The three men were all ripped and solid. And tall. Her eyes were at shoulder level or below for all of them, though she wouldn't look straight at them. She was too embarrassed at having stumbled into Mr. X on the way in. There was one other person in the elevator, a woman in a business suit who had a magazine in one hand and

2

seemed to be reading it, but Lindsay noticed she kept glancing at the men with interest.

A few floors up the elevator stopped and a young guy in a T-shirt and jeans got on. The three men and Lindsay shifted to the side, pushing her closer to Mr. X.

"Hey, Connor. Travis. You must be busy packing for the move."

"Just finished. We move out tomorrow morning," one of Mr. X's companions said. "Now it's time for a swim."

The man who initiated the conversation laughed as the elevator doors opened again. "Hope it goes well." Then he disappeared down the hall as the doors closed.

A couple floors later, another four people got on. They exchanged polite hellos with the men as they pressed in closer to make room. With Mr. X in the corner and his friends beside her, Lindsay felt like she was surrounded by a wall of muscular male flesh. She could feel the heat of their bodies.

Tingles quivered through her and her imagination conjured delectable images. *Mr. X wrapped his hand around her waist and drew her tightly to his body as his lips brushed her neck. Then he turned her around while one of his friends stepped behind her. She felt both their hard bodies pressing against her. The third man stroked her hair, then nuzzled her ear as Mr. X claimed her lips with an eager passion, his tongue driving into her mouth.*

Oh, God, the images were so hot her body began to ache with need. Imagining the feel of Mr. X's solid body pressed to hers, a huge erection pushing against her, his friend behind her also sporting a raging hard-on that pushed against her ass, sent her hormones spinning out of control.

Lips traced along her neck, sending tingles fluttering along her spine.

The images changed and she felt all three of their naked bodies entwined with hers. Moving against her. Touching her everywhere. Kissing her everywhere. The sensations were muddled. She had no sense of what or how, just hard male bodies—sexy bodies—giving her intense pleasure.

The elevator doors opened and her eyelids flickered, then opened wide.

Oh, God, she'd lost track of what was going on around her. Only two other people remained in the elevator besides her and the three half-naked men, and those two people were getting off. The doors closed behind them and panic set in as she realized she was alone in the elevator with these Adonis-like specimens of manhood.

She stared at the elevator buttons, willing her floor to come up soon. Then she realized she was still standing close to them in the corner of a practically empty elevator, so she shifted forward a little.

She half expected Mr. X to draw her back, then pull her into his arms, then all of them to ravish her. Or, if she was stuck here much longer, she might ravish them.

Who said she didn't have sexual fantasies? Though they'd never been this potent.

The elevator stopped and she impatiently waited for the doors to open, then she fled the small, confined space.

4

———

Erik watched the gorgeous young blonde woman hurry down the hall as the elevator doors closed, his gaze locked firmly on her deliciously swaying ass. He hadn't gotten much of a look at her face, but her body was curved in all the right places. And her reactions to him and his two friends, Travis and Connor, had delighted him. She'd pretended not to notice them after their first interaction, but it was clear that she was totally mesmerized by their presence.

He was glad they'd decided to take this break from packing up Travis and Connor's apartment to go for a swim.

"Damn, she was sexy as hell," Connor said.

"True that," said Travis.

Erik nodded absently. She was also sweet and a little shy. Had low self-esteem. And had a burning inferno of passion hidden deep inside. And he would love to be the one to let it loose. Along with Connor and Travis.

"I thought you were off men."

Lindsay stopped swirling her fingertip around the rim of her wineglass and glanced at her best friend, Jill. Lindsay had just told her about the hot fantasies that had burst through her during the elevator ride.

"I'm not on them." Her words immediately triggered a hot image of her straddling Mr. X. If his manhood was proportional to the rest of him, it would be huge. She could almost feel it, and couldn't help imagining moving up and down on him.

Jill laughed. "Lindsay, you're doing it again, aren't you?"

Lindsay sent her friend a guilty glance. Her burning cheeks had to be a dead giveaway.

"Well, I can't help it. Those guys were big and hot and . . . sexy. I barely got a glimpse of their faces, but they were ripped."

Jill placed a bowl of cashews on the table, then sat down with her glass of wine.

"Well, hey, I didn't say I disapprove. Maybe we should try to find out who these guys are." She grinned. "I could ask around."

"Someone mentioned their names. At least, two of them. Connor and . . . uh, Travis."

"Connor and Travis? I know them. They hang out at the pool a lot and you know how I love to go swimming. They're really nice guys." Jill smiled. "As for the third man . . . there's this other guy who visits them frequently and he's just as smoking hot as they are. No wonder your imagination ran wild." Her eyes twinkled. "You know, I could introduce you. Then maybe you could live out those hot fantasies."

"Are you saying I should go off with three guys and have sex?"

Jill laughed. "Well, if the opportunity presented itself."

Lindsay sipped her wine and laughed. "I think I'll keep that particular fantasy just that. A fantasy." She sipped her wine. "Oh, and speaking of fantasies, over lunch, Audrey accused me of not having sexual fantasies."

"You're kidding? Why would she even mention anything about"—Jill's eyes widened and she held her hand in front of her mouth in mock mortification—"you know . . . sex!"

Lindsay giggled. "Well, I guess she'd rather go there than admit she'd been wrong."

Audrey had set her up with Glen, insisting he was the perfect man for her. Since he was well-educated, made a lot of money, and was as handsome as sin, clearly in Audrey's mind the fault had to lie with Lindsay.

In retrospect, Lindsay couldn't believe she'd gone along with meeting him in the first place, but Audrey had been insistent and Lindsay had been suffering a dry spell in the romance department. In fact, she'd been out with a string of losers over the past few years. Was it just her, or did guys seem to be more interested in having regular sex than an actual relationship?

At first, Glen had seemed quite promising. Charming and attentive. After about six months, however, his interest seemed to wane and he became distant and increasingly critical. Lindsay was determined to make it work, though. Clearly, more determined than he was.

"Just remember. You decided a long time ago not to let what Audrey thinks get you down. If you listened to her, you'd have changed jobs long ago and moved farther out of the city so you could have a bigger apartment. But then you'd be living her idea of what your life should be, not yours."

It was true. Her father might love the woman, and Lindsay would do her best to keep peace, but being raised by a woman who simply did not understand her had been hard. And Dad had never seemed to notice the strife between them. Now that she was an adult, she would do the occasional lunch with Audrey, but Lindsay had long ago given up on trying to make things work between them.

"You know," Jill said with an impish grin on her face, "I think you should reconsider meeting Connor and Travis. I could set you up on a wild, sexy weekend with them. Afterward, you can shock the pants off Audrey by explaining that you decided to take her advice and then tell her all about it."

"Jill, you're terrible." But Lindsay giggled anyway.

But the thought of those big, sexy bodies set her insides quivering. She was sure they would star in her dreams for a long time to come.

Three weeks later, Lindsay got off the bus and walked the block to her own apartment building. It was smaller and far less glamorous than her parents', but she liked it.

She turned the key in her mailbox and pulled out the handful of envelopes from inside, then glanced through the small stack as she rode the elevator to her floor. A bill from the electric company, something from her dentist—

probably reminding her about her next checkup, a couple of flyers, and . . .

How unusual. She gazed at the linen envelope with a satin ribbon tied around it and only her first name written on the front. She didn't recognize the handwriting, but it looked masculine. There was no return address.

She walked down the hall to her apartment and dropped her mail on the table in the small entryway while she took off her shoes, then picked up the envelope again. She untied the ribbon and pulled out a white card with the words "You are invited . . ." in silver letters on the front. She opened it to read the message in script inside.

To a magical fantasy weekend with three attentive men who will satisfy your every sexual whim.

This had to be a joke.

Below the message were details including the date, an address, and a map. The invitation was for next weekend and the address was downtown, right off the river.

Why would someone send her this? Then it occurred to her. Jill had kidded her for days about the elevator incident. This was probably from her. They'd been talking about setting up a girls' weekend away for months now, but had never gotten around to it. It would be just like Jill to do something like this to make it happen. The fact that the location was right here in the city was odd, but maybe Jill had found a good deal on a vacation condo or something and had set up a staycation. Whatever her friend had planned, Lindsay hoped it involved a day spa and a nice long massage.

She peered in the envelope and found a key card inside. A little yellow sticky note said "Unit 2101." Jill had a friend who asked her to house-sit her condo sometimes. Jill had probably asked if she could borrow the place to make it feel like a real weekend getaway.

Lindsay smiled. A change of setting would do her good. She and Jill could just kick back and enjoy themselves.

She dropped the envelope on the dining room table as she headed for the kitchen to start dinner. She grinned. She wouldn't mention anything to Jill about receiving the invitation. Keep her guessing whether she'd show up or not. It would serve her right for teasing her so mercilessly.

As Lindsay walked toward the entrance of the tall, glittering building a doorman stepped toward her, smiling.

"May I help you, ma'am?"

"Um, yes. I've been invited to unit 2101."

"Your name?"

"Lindsay Reed."

He smiled. "Of course, Ms. Reed." He opened the glass door. "Just walk past the elevators, then take a right. The private elevator is down that corridor. You have a key card?"

She nodded. The card had been included with the invitation and was now in her purse.

Private elevator?

She stepped from the humid heat of the afternoon into the cool, air-conditioned lobby. She walked toward the elevators, her high heels clacking on the glossy marble floors, then turned right as directed. At the end, she found a single elevator door with a slot for a key card. She set down her overnight bag and grabbed the crystal heart on the zipper tag of her new, dark purple purse and pulled it open, retrieved the card, and slid it into the slot. The doors opened immediately.

Inside the roomy elevator was a cushioned bench. The walls were mirrored and the floor covered with soft carpet. She stepped inside and set her bag on the bench. The doors closed and the elevator began moving upward.

The building was very high class. She began to doubt it was the friend whose apartment Jill house-sat. Maybe Jill's boss had let her use it for the weekend. The woman owned her own company and had a big house in the country. Lindsay wouldn't be surprised if she kept an apartment in the city, too.

Would Jill be at the apartment already? If she wasn't, how would Lindsay get in? Unless the key card opened the apartment door, too, which was what she'd originally assumed.

The elevator slowed, then came to a stop and the doors opened. Lindsay's eyes widened as she stepped out of the elevator into the biggest, most luxurious apartment she'd ever seen. The elevator doors closed behind her and she stepped farther into the entryway and glanced around the large living room beyond with plush leather couches and armchairs, a large marble fireplace, a huge flat-screen television, and a large window overlooking the city.

Lindsay took off her shoes and placed them on the ceramic tiled floor beside the hall closet, then set down her purse beside them and stepped into the living room, her feet sinking into the thick carpet. It wasn't as cool as in the lobby, but with a soft breeze washing through the place from the open windows, it was a comfortable temperature.

She padded across the room to the hallway in search of the bedrooms. Five doors spanned the hallway, only two open. The one at the far end of the hall seemed to be a bathroom, the other was the first door on the left. She shrugged and decided that must be the guest room. Inside she found a large queen bed with white bedding and a dark chocolate coverlet across the bottom of the bed which matched the leather headboard. She set her overnight bag on the coverlet as she glanced around at the sumptuous room. Green and brown accent pillows topped the bed and facing the window sat a brown leather chaise longue with accent pillows that matched those on the bed. The bedside tables and dresser were a glossy mahogany and behind the double folding doors must be a very large closet.

She crossed the room and peeked out the window, then sucked in a breath. Right outside was a private patio with teak chairs around a glass table shaded under an umbrella and lounge chairs skirting a private pool.

———

Travis pushed the button to the penthouse and the doors to the elevator closed.

"I might never get used to this place," Connor said. "Private elevator. Luxury penthouse."

"I don't think I should get used to it."

Connor nudged his elbow. "Look, Erik inherited this place and he wants us to live with him. It wouldn't make sense to turn him down just because we couldn't afford the rent on a place like this. Erik really doesn't care about stuff like that."

"I know. I didn't turn it down."

"Yeah, but I had to practically twist your arm."

It was true. Connor really wanted the two of them to move in with Erik, and Travis wanted that, too. The three of them had a solid relationship and Travis wanted them all to be together as much as Connor and Erik did. He just wished it had been somewhere he could afford. It was important to him to pull his own weight. He'd been living on his own since he was seventeen and he'd never relied on anyone. Financially, anyway. Since he'd moved in with Connor several years ago, he had learned to rely on Connor for emotional support. And for sex, of course. Erik came along later, but the three of them had forged a strong, intimate relationship together.

"Listen, when we get upstairs, let's go for a quick swim before Lindsay arrives," Connor suggested.

Travis' stomach knotted, despite the thought of a nice

swim in the heated pool. He was looking forward to a wild weekend sharing a sexy woman with his two friends, but it was the first time they'd had a woman to a place they all shared. It would be a little strange, especially since he still didn't feel quite settled.

"She'll be here soon, so we don't really have time."

The elevator arrived at the rooftop apartment and the doors opened.

At a noise in the other room, Lindsay turned her head. She walked toward the door, straining to hear. It sounded like the elevator doors opening. Well, now that Jill had arrived, she could find out what was going on.

"It looks like our guest is here," someone said in the other room, but it was a man's voice.

An unfamiliar voice. Lindsay stiffened. Why had Jill invited a man?

"How do you know?" another man said.

"Right there. Unless Erik's taken to cross-dressing, those aren't his shoes and purse."

Someone chuckled. "Erik texted me to say he'd be late, so they're definitely not his."

"So he wasn't here when she arrived? Let's go find her."

Panic rose in Lindsay. Oh, God, the invitation had been the real deal. She'd been invited to come and party— sexually—with three men. Three *strange* men.

TWO

Lindsay's heart thundered in her chest. They were coming to find her.

She pushed the door closed very quietly, then stared at it, wondering what to do next.

Was this Jill's doing? Had she gone ahead and set up this fantasy weekend? Lindsay couldn't believe Jill would do that, but there was no other reasonable explanation.

These guys believed she'd come here to live out her sexual fantasy with them.

Her head started to spin and she drew in a deep breath.

How could she possibly get out of here without coming face-to-face with them?

They think I'm here to have sex with them. Her cheeks burned.

She sucked in another breath. *Calm down.*

Once she explained it was all a mistake, that she

didn't want to be here . . . well, it would be embarrassing, but she just had to tell them. Then she'd leave.

She pressed her ear to the door. She couldn't hear any footsteps, but with the lovely plush carpet, she wouldn't.

"It looks like she's in the bedroom."

She jumped at the voice outside the door.

"Should we knock?" the other man asked.

"No, she might be having a nap. Or changing. She'll come out when she's ready." His voice seemed to be moving away. "For now, let's just go for a swim."

She sucked in a breath of air, relieved at her reprieve, then she glanced at the window. Oh, man, they'd be walking right by that window. They'd be able to see her in here.

She raced to the window, noticing the wooden horizontal blinds stacked closed at the top, and grabbed the string on the right, then released the catch. The blinds swept down over the open window, the horizontal slats at an angle to let light in. She saw two men walk toward the pool only a couple of yards from the window. It was too late to close the blinds all the way without being noticed. Could they see her?

But the angle of the slats provided only a small opening between each. She could see out, but they'd need to peer straight in to see her.

She crouched down and watched them. They were tall and muscular, just like the men on the elevator. She had been so self-conscious about tripping into Mr. X, she had barely gotten a glimpse of their faces, but she was pretty sure this was Connor and Travis.

They hadn't even gone to change first. They both wore jeans and T-shirts. And, good heavens, they were absolutely gorgeous. Both were tall and broad-shouldered. One had long, dark hair hanging below his muscular shoulders. His eyes were dark brown, his nose slender and his lips full. She couldn't help imagining those lips pressed to hers, his arms around her. The other had short, layered, dark blond hair with spiky bangs and a strong, masculine jaw. His smile was wide, showing straight, white teeth.

The one on the left peeled off his shirt and tossed it aside. His chest was broad and sculpted. He unbuttoned his jeans and dropped them to the deck, then stepped out of them, wearing only bright yellow boxers with a happy face. He tucked his thumbs under the waistband.

"Really, Connor? You're going to strip naked? Don't you think that would make our guest uncomfortable?"

Connor shrugged. "She's probably sleeping. But even if she isn't"—he tugged down his boxers and Lindsay's eyes widened at the size of his cock—"why not give her a preview of what to expect?"

The other man chuckled. "Yeah? With that big column, you might just frighten her away."

"Really?" Connor wrapped his hand around his cock and stroked it. "You and Erik have never found it particularly frightening."

"As generous as your proportions are, Erik has you beat. And me?" Travis shrugged. "What can I say? I like big cock."

My God, if this Erik guy had a bigger penis than that . . . A part of her would love to stick around just to see it.

Connor glanced at her window and she ducked, her heart pounding, though more from the effect of seeing his big cock and the sudden longing to wrap her hand around it, just as his was, than from fear of being seen.

"Show me, Travis." Connor's cock had started to swell.

The other man—Travis—walked toward him, shedding his T-shirt, then jeans as he approached, revealing a sexy, tanned frame, just as muscle-bound as the man named Connor. He did not remove his pinstriped navy boxers, though, leaving Lindsay a little disappointed.

He grabbed one of the patio chairs beside Connor and pulled it in front of him, then sat down.

"I'm going to suck that big cock of yours, just like the little lady in the other room will do when we're all together." Travis wrapped his hand around Connor's rigid shaft and stroked. "Her pretty little lips will wrap around your hard cock and she'll glide it into her mouth."

"God, yeah. Now stop talking and suck some cock." Connor wrapped his hand around Travis' head and drew him to his crotch.

Travis chuckled, then rested his head against Connor's pelvis and licked his shaven balls. He stroked the big cock, then drew back and pressed the cock-head to his mouth. Connor groaned as Travis hesitated, the mushroom-shaped flesh pressed against his lips. Travis chuckled again, then opened and swallowed the other man into his mouth.

"God damn, that feels good," Connor said.

He grabbed Travis' head again and pulled him forward. The long shaft disappeared into Travis' mouth as he glided forward until he pressed tight to Connor's crotch.

Lindsay couldn't believe Travis had taken him so deep. How did he do that without gagging?

Connor groaned and murmured as Travis bobbed up and down on his cock, swallowing it deep inside each time, his hands cupping Connor's hard, muscular buttocks. Then Connor stiffened and groaned loudly, his face contorting as he came to climax.

Lindsay's breasts swelled and her insides ached with need. As she watched the flaccid cock slip from Travis' lips, she wished it was still hard and that she had the guts to march out there right now and climb aboard.

Connor grabbed Travis and pulled him to his feet, then kissed him. Hot and hard. Their masculine mouths consumed each other. Connor's hands glided down Travis' back, circling the muscles, then he cupped the man's hard, boxer-clad butt and squeezed.

Connor grabbed the hem and pushed the boxers down. As much as Travis had let on that his cock didn't match Connor's in size, that was anything but the truth. The guy was just as long, if not quite as thick.

"You just don't want to skinny-dip alone," Travis said as he kicked his boxers aside.

"Screw that. I just want to suck you off. Now lie down on the diving board, legs spread."

Lindsay's breath caught. Would he talk to her that way? Coarse and demanding. Directing her to do things—sexual things—for his pleasure?

Travis walked to the diving board and lay back on it, his legs wide open straddling the board, his knees bent and his feet flat on the stone deck that surrounded the pool. His head was toward the water. Connor sat on the other end of the board, near Travis' knees, then he grasped Travis' cock and squeezed, then stroked.

Lindsay could imagine that big, hard cock in her hand as she stroked it up and down. Connor leaned forward and licked the cock, then he dove down on it with gusto.

As she watched his mouth bounce up and down on the long, hard erection, her insides thrumming with need, she realized she was wasting valuable time. Because with the two of them out there, totally preoccupied, she could make a dash for the door without being discovered.

No confrontation. No awkwardness.

She dragged her attention from the extremely arousing scene outside and sauntered across the room, then pressed her ear to the door and listened. When she didn't hear anything, she opened it slowly, peering out to ensure no one was waiting in the hallway. When she saw the coast was clear, she pulled the door open all the way and tiptoed into the hallway. She peered around the corner into the large sitting area facing the window. No sign of the two men outside.

She walked faster, heading toward the elevator, then froze as she noticed a humming sound. Oh, God, the elevator. The doors parted and her jaw fell open as a drop-dead gorgeous man in police uniform stepped out.

His gaze locked on her and her heart stopped. His eyes were so blue. The color of the sky at twilight. And she couldn't help noticing his strong, square jaw, his classic nose, high cheekbones . . . and his sexy lips.

And the glinting badge on his shirt.

Erik hadn't realized just how beautiful she was, with her full, pink lips, bright blue-gray eyes, and shimmering golden hair that flowed well past her shoulders.

"Oh, um . . . hello, Officer," she said.

"Hi. Is there something wrong?" The woman was clearly flustered. And he sensed slightly aroused.

"Um . . . No, not really, I was just on my way out."

Why would she come all the way here, then leave?

Then again, women weren't always rational. He'd learned that the hard way. In the half dozen or so serious relationships he'd had, they'd all ended with the woman walking out. Why? Because he knew them too well. He *satisfied* them too well. They didn't want someone who could read them as well as he could. In his book, that was not rational.

"I thought you came for the weekend," he said.

Her eyes widened. "Oh, my God. You're the third man."

"That's right." He smiled reassuringly, wondering if his uniform was intimidating her.

"Look, there's been a bit of a mistake—"

At the sound of Travis and Connor's voices behind her, she spun around. At the sight of the two men walking into the room—Travis with a towel wrapped around his waist and Connor with his towel draped over his shoulder, leaving him essentially naked—her face blossomed with color. Their broad shoulders and glistening, muscular chests were a sight to see, but her gaze dropped to Connor's big, dangling penis. Then shot away.

Had they started without him? Whatever had happened between them had clearly scared her off.

"Well, here's our lovely guest, and it seems she's met Erik," Connor said.

Travis jabbed Connor in the ribs. "Uh, Connor, you're making her uncomfortable."

"Oh, sorry." Connor grinned as he tugged the towel from his shoulder, then wrapped it around his waist. He pushed his dark, blond hair from his face, then stepped toward her and held out his hand. "Hi, there. My name's Connor Jackson."

"Haven't you already met?" Erik asked.

"No, Lindsay was in her room when we arrived," Travis said, "so we went out for a swim."

Three

Lindsay stared at Connor's outstretched arm and hesitantly placed her hand in his. His big, strong fingers enveloped hers as he shook her hand gently, then squeezed. Her gaze shifted to his, and locked onto his hazel eyes, glittering with golden specks. Heat coursed through her as she remembered him holding his big cock in his hand, then later wrapping it around the other man's. He smiled, as if he knew what she was thinking, and that she'd been watching them.

Finally, he released her hand and the other man stepped toward her, his hand outstretched.

"Travis Blake," he said as she placed her hand in his. His full lips pulled up in a warm, welcoming smile. He shook her hand, his chocolate brown eyes simmering with heat.

"I haven't introduced myself yet," the police officer said, stepping toward her. "My name's Erik Hamilton."

"Hi, I'm Lindsay."

When she took Erik's hand, a wave of heat washed through her, and she imagined his arms sweeping around her, pulling her tight to his hard, muscular body while his mouth devoured hers.

She could see her need mirrored in his mesmerizing, deep blue eyes and she could feel herself being drawn deeper into the fantasy, longing for more. Wanting him to pull her into his arms in real life, to kiss the bejesus out of her, then start to explore her body with that sexy mouth of his.

When he released her hand, she just stared at him, slightly rattled at his effect on her.

"Lindsay was just telling me there's been some kind of mistake."

"Oh? Did you see us out by the pool?" Travis asked, his eyes narrowing.

Oh, damn. Erik felt a pang in his gut.

Lindsay nodded and the warmth dissipated from Travis' eyes.

Now the pieces fell into place. Lindsay had been in her room when the guys arrived, so they went out for a swim. But it wasn't just a swim. Now Travis believed that Lindsay had been repulsed by the sight of two men having sex.

"I'm going to change," Travis said flatly and strode away.

Connor and Erik exchanged a glance. Connor had figured it out, too. Erik wasn't convinced that Lindsay had a problem with the guys being intimate, but Travis had a chip on his shoulder about these things.

Connor turned his attention back to Lindsay. "Are you having second thoughts?"

"No, not second thoughts." She dragged her gaze from Travis' retreating back, looking a bit perplexed. "I thought the invitation was actually from my friend. A joke invitation to a girls' weekend."

"Well, that's unfortunate," Connor said.

"So you never intended to accept the invitation?" Erik asked.

"No. I mean . . . I don't know any of you and . . . well, it's kind of wild, the idea of me coming here to . . . um . . . be with three men."

So he was right. Her leaving had nothing to do with seeing Connor and Travis together. In fact, Erik suspected that the sight of them together had actually turned her on. That would explain the arousal he'd sensed in her when he arrived.

Right from the first time he'd seen her in the elevator, he could tell she was a sensuous woman who had an active and exciting imagination. It had been a wild ride up that day, with sexual fantasies swirling through his head. His cock had hardened and he'd been tempted to stop the elevator when the last set of people got off and offer to satiate her need. With all three of them.

Of course, doing that would have been crazy, but he

was sure she had been as mesmerized as he. And even now, he sensed that she was definitely curious. Maybe she just needed a little coaxing.

"I understand that this situation is a bit overwhelming," he said, "but you came all the way here. Why don't you stay for a swim and maybe talk a little? Get to know us. Then if you still want to leave, I'll drive you home."

"I don't have a bathing suit with me. And I don't want to mislead you. I am not going to stay for a . . . uh . . . fantasy weekend. My friend Jill set this up, right? Because I don't know what she told you, or what she was thinking to arrange this in the first place. But I think there's been a *really* big misunderstanding."

"We get that the whole sexual fantasy thing is off the table," Connor said, "but I have a suggestion. Why don't you and Erik go out for the evening? You can talk and get to know each other. I sense there's some smoking hot chemistry between you. If there is, maybe you'll want to explore it a little more. If not, then all you've lost is a few hours of your time."

And that would give Connor some time to talk to Travis and calm him down.

"That's a great idea," Erik said, stepping toward her. "What do you say?"

The heat of her soft, feminine body drew him like a warm magnet, and he sensed he was having the same effect on her.

She gazed at him, and he could tell she was more than a little tempted, but still she hesitated.

"He's a cop, so you know you can trust him," Connor chimed in. "And you've got to admit, that uniform's hot."

The closeness of his body, especially in the uniform, was definitely making Lindsay hot. There was no denying that the whole situation was completely crazy, but her gut told her to live on the wild side just this once.

"I know a great little place just a few blocks from here," Erik said. "We could walk. Then afterward, I'll drive you home."

He was the hottest guy she'd ever seen and he was asking her on a date. *You don't know him*, the voice of reason said. *Don't you want to change that?* another more adventurous voice chimed in.

"All right."

A wide smile spread across his face, lighting his midnight eyes. "Just give me a minute to change."

Erik turned and headed toward the hall, then disappeared around the corner. She leaned over and pulled on her shoes.

"Well, here we are. Alone at last."

She started and turned to Connor, who still wore only a towel draped around his waist. Thoughts of his big, heavy penis dangling beneath the covering wafted through her brain.

He chuckled. "Come on. I'll get you a drink." He turned and walked toward a door off the dining room.

She hesitated, then realized it would be silly to just stand by the elevator for ten minutes waiting for Erik to return. She followed him, her gaze drifting to the towel on his hips that slipped lower and lower as he walked. Her breath caught as the towel started to drop free, but he caught it and tucked the end securely into place again.

She followed him through the door into a huge kitchen with granite counters, stainless steel appliances, tall stools at the counter, and a table and chairs in a generous eating area near a huge window with a great view of the pool.

Connor opened the fridge. "We've got beer and juice. Or I could make you a margarita or something."

"A juice, please."

He twisted the top off a bottle and handed it to her, then opened one for himself.

"This is a really nice place," she said, glancing around at the beautiful dark wood cabinets, black shiny countertops, and the glossy hardwood floor.

"We like it."

She sat on one of the high stools at the counter and sipped her drink.

"Do you all live here together?"

He leaned against the counter and smiled. "Yeah. We moved in about three weeks ago. Before that, Travis and I were roommates. Now it's the three of us."

"Three of us?" Erik said as he walked into the room, wearing dark jeans and a striped cotton shirt. "Are you joining us, Connor?"

Connor chuckled. "I wouldn't think of it." He grabbed

his juice and walked to the door. "I think Travis and I will catch a movie tonight, then head over to that new club. But I'd better put on some clothes first."

As Connor disappeared out the doorway, Lindsay stood up, ready to leave.

"Go ahead and finish your drink. There's no rush." Erik sat beside her at the counter.

"Connor was just telling me you all moved in here recently."

Erik glanced around. "Yeah. We're still getting used to the place."

"It's a gorgeous apartment. And I can't believe you have a pool right outside the door. Is it just for your use?"

"That's right. It's totally private." He turned toward her, leaning his elbow on the counter. "Speaking of which, I assume that earlier you saw Connor and Travis outside doing more than swimming."

She pursed her lips and nodded. "I'm sorry, I didn't mean to intrude on their privacy."

"Not at all. I'm sure they didn't care at all that you saw them. Travis was just reacting to the fact you were leaving and I'm sure he thought it was because you saw them and were making"—he shrugged—"I don't know, some kind of judgment about them."

Her chest tightened. "Oh, no. Not at all. That's not why I was leaving."

"I know. I just wanted to explain why Travis acted that way. Don't worry, Connor will explain the mix-up to him."

"Hey, you two." Connor poked his head in the door. "Travis and I are leaving now. Want to ride down with us?"

Lindsay took a last sip of her drink, then followed Connor to the entrance. Travis stood inside the elevator holding the doors open. Connor grabbed her purse from the floor and handed it to her.

Lindsay preceded him into the elevator. She felt tiny standing amongst the three tall men. The doors closed and the elevator began to move. Erik stood at her side with Connor and Travis behind them. At the heat of their bodies so close to her, her insides quivered. They were so hot and sexy. She drew in a deep breath, trying to suppress the steamy images fluttering through her brain. Of Connor stepping forward until his hard body pressed the length of her. Of Travis sliding close beside her and stroking her hair from her face, his fingers trailing lightly across her temple, then his lips nuzzling her ear. Of Erik stepping in front of her, then taking her in his arms and capturing her lips in a passionate kiss.

Erik coughed and she glanced up at him. He smiled at her, a twinkle in his eyes, and she could almost believe he could see the images in her head. Even though she knew that was impossible, her cheeks flushed.

Erik continued to smile at her, as if he knew just what she was thinking.

Damn it, what came over her in elevators? At least, in elevators with these three men.

When the doors opened, she practically lurched into the lobby.

Connor and Travis said good-bye as they headed for the elevator to the parking garage and Erik walked with her to the front door.

They stepped into the warm evening air and walked along the sidewalk. It was still early on a summer's evening so the sun wouldn't set for a while yet. They walked by a restaurant with planters of pink and purple petunias out front, then crossed at a light and continued down another block.

"Here it is." Erik opened the door for her and she entered the welcoming cool air of the bar.

Soft music was playing and she noticed a dance floor near the back. The hostess guided them to a quiet table, then a waitress came by and took their drink order.

"You live in a really nice neighborhood," Lindsay said. It was definitely a prime area. She wondered how they could afford such an extravagant place in such a posh area.

"We like it. We haven't had much time to explore yet. We're still settling in."

The waitress brought their drinks.

"So why don't you tell me a bit about yourself?" Erik said.

"Oh, well, I've lived here all my life. I went away to college, but came back right after that. My father and stepmother live in a big house in the suburbs, but I prefer to live downtown close to the office."

"What do you like to do in your spare time?"

"I like movies and books, but I'm also pretty active. I like snow skiing, not that I get a lot of chances to do that, and I really like the water. Swimming, boating, going to the beach."

He smiled. "That's why you like our pool so much."

"Yeah. I'd love to have a pool right outside the door like that." She swirled her finger around the rim of her glass. "So what about you?"

"I grew up in New York. I moved out here about eight years ago, just before I joined the force."

"You're a long way from home. Do you miss your family?"

"No. Connor and Travis are the only family I need."

His expression closed up as soon as she mentioned his family. She'd have loved to ask him more about them but sensed he wouldn't appreciate it.

"Hey there, do you mind if we join you?"

She glanced up and saw Connor approaching the table, Travis by his side.

"It turns out we have about twenty minutes to kill before the movie."

Erik glanced at her questioningly, and she nodded. The two men sat down, Connor beside her and Travis beside Erik.

The waitress stopped by to take their drink orders.

Then the four of them chatted for a bit about the movie the guys were going to go see.

"So how long have you all known each other?" Lindsay asked.

"Travis and I have known each other for seven years," Connor answered, "and we met Erik five years ago."

"Connor and I met at the university," Travis said, "then became roommates after we graduated. We met Erik at a party."

"Yeah, you could say that." Erik turned to her, a big grin on his face. "I was actually on duty and came to break up a fight at said party."

Her gaze flicked to Connor and Travis. "Were you two in the fight?"

"No, we were trying to break it up when he arrived," Travis said.

Erik nodded. "They'd been drinking so they weren't being all that effective, but everything settled down when my partner and I arrived, so we didn't have to arrest anyone. I saw these two in the coffee shop near the campus a few times after that," he continued, "and we got to talking, and wound up becoming friends."

Connor chuckled. "And more."

"Well, you've seen the man in his uniform." Travis grinned.

She loved that they were so open and easy about their sexual interest in each other.

Lindsay smiled. "It's true. He does look pretty good in that uniform."

The thought of him in his dark blue shirt, stretched taut over his big chest, badge gleaming, and a look of authority in his eyes set her blood simmering. She imagined him ordering her to turn around and rest her hands on the table, then running his hands up and down her body, searching her. His fingers would glide over her breasts and pat them. Her nipples hardened at the thought of his big, masculine hands squeezing lightly before continuing down her hips, then over her ass.

Erik's gaze shifted to hers, and his eyes seemed to darken.

"Hey, how can you sit here with such a beautiful woman and not ask her to dance?" Travis asked.

"That's a great idea," Erik said, his gaze boring into her.

She shifted her focus from Erik's searing gaze to Connor. "But you two are only here for a little while." Although Lindsay would love to be in Erik's arms right now, she didn't want to be rude.

"Forget about that," Connor said. "We have to get going anyway." He drained his beer and stood up. "Ready, Travis?"

Travis stood up, too. "You two have fun." Then he followed Connor from the bar.

"Well, would you like to dance?" Erik asked.

She smiled and extended her hand.

He took it in his and led her to the dance floor. His big fingers wrapped around hers sent heat thrumming through her. He took her in his arms, drawing her close to his solid body, and she settled her hand on his broad, muscular shoulder. Her breath caught. He was so big and so . . . masculine. She felt tiny and very feminine in his strong arms. He guided her around the dance floor with a masterful authority and she found herself longing to be mastered by him in other ways.

After a couple of songs, they returned to the table and had another drink, then when a slow, romantic song came on, he asked her to dance again. She was feeling more relaxed with him and she rested her head against his shoulder. He held her close, his solid chest tight against her. Her insides melted at the heat of him and she had to suppress her desire to nuzzle his neck.

"You feel so good against me," he murmured.

"Mmm, you, too."

His lips nuzzled her temple and shivers danced along her spine. After a couple more songs, her body was quivering with need. She couldn't help imagining his lips moving along her cheek, then finding her lips. His tongue slipping into her mouth and exploring while his hard body pressed even tighter against her.

"You know," he murmured against her ear, "Connor and Travis will be out for several hours. The penthouse is empty if you'd like to go back for a drink. We could sit out by the pool. Maybe go for a swim."

"That sounds like a great idea." Though swimming was the last thing on her mind.

He led her from the floor and returned to their seats. He tossed some money on the table, then she grabbed her purse and followed him from the bar. The warm air outside did nothing to cool down the desire burning within her. Soon they were in his building with the elevator doors closing behind them.

He gazed at her, his eyes like burning embers, but he didn't make a move toward her. The previous two times she'd been in an elevator with him and his two friends, steamy fantasies had danced through her head. Now that she'd felt his body against her for real on the dance floor, and experienced his lips on her skin, she could hardly contain herself. She quivered with desire.

But he was holding back. Being a perfect gentleman.

The hell with this. She stepped forward and rested her hands on his muscular shoulders, then lifted her face to his.

"Kiss me."

Four

Lindsay watched his eyes darken as his arms wrapped around her, then his mouth captured hers in a passionate kiss. His lips were firm and confident as they moved on hers, then his tongue glided into her mouth and swirled inside, taking her breath away.

Too soon, the elevator doors opened, but he scooped her up and carried her into the apartment, then headed toward the couch.

"No. The bedroom." She knew where this was going and didn't want the other two men walking in on them.

He smiled broadly and changed course. In moments, he set her on his bed.

She gazed up at him, her breathing erratic, and started to unbutton her blouse. He knelt in front of her.

"Let me."

Slowly, he unfastened her buttons, one by one, revealing the swell of her breasts. When he was done, he parted the fabric. Her nipples hardened as his gaze ran over her blue lace—clad breasts, his eyes full of admiration. He leaned in and nuzzled her neck, then gazed down at her breasts again.

"You're so beautiful."

The words made her feel beautiful, and so did the way he was staring at the outline of her swelling nipples.

She slipped the blouse from her shoulders and let it fall to the floor, then stood up and unfastened her jeans. He watched with avid interest as she dropped them to the floor, revealing her tiny, blue lace panties.

"Now you," she said.

Lindsay licked her lips, longing to see the broad muscular chest hugged by the striped cotton fabric.

Standing in front of her, he unfastened his top button, then the second, revealing tanned flesh. Her throat went dry as he continued downward. He dropped the shirt over his shoulders and let it slip away, revealing a broad, muscular chest and tight ridges of muscle defining his abs. She stared at him, salivating, her insides flashing with heat like a wildfire.

He unfastened his pants and pushed them to the ground, then stepped out of them. She stared at the huge bulge in his boxers, showing her exactly how much he wanted her. She almost giggled in delight.

He stepped closer and stroked her hair behind her ear. Her nipples swelled at his touch, and she longed for him to caress them. He cupped her face, then his lips meshed with hers.

Heat blazed through her and her inner passage clenched as she longed for his cock to be inside her. His tongue slid along the seam of her mouth and she opened, then her tongue dodged out to meet his. They tangled together, then he pulled her closer as he drove into her mouth. She ran her fingers through his short hair and she murmured as sweet yearning pulsed through her.

When he released her mouth, she sucked in air. He stroked down her neck to the swell of her breast, then glided his finger along the edge of the lace cup of her bra. She wanted him to slip underneath and touch her naked flesh. He dipped his head to kiss her neck, his lips fluttering along her skin.

Behind him, she noticed his dark blue police hat sitting on the top of his armoire and images of him when he arrived at the penthouse in his uniform sent heat thrumming through her. He had been so big and sexy and . . . authoritative, standing there in his blue uniform, with his brimmed hat and his badge.

He lifted his head and gazed at her. "You like the fact I'm a police officer."

"How did you know that's what I was thinking?"

He turned to the armoire and grabbed his hat. "You're looking at this, right?" He placed it on his head and her breath caught.

She nodded, unable to utter a word as he approached her. He was a cop. His big, broad chest was naked. A huge erection pushed at his boxers. And he was about to have sex with her.

He grinned. "You know, it's okay. Cops are allowed to have sex. Especially when they're off duty."

She nodded again.

He laughed and pulled her into his arms, then captured her lips. She could barely catch her breath as his tongue stormed her mouth, his arms tightening to crush her against his solid chest.

When he released her, she gazed up at him and licked her lips.

His smile faded as he took on a serious expression and backed her toward the bed. "Ma'am, you're acting very suspicious."

She stopped when she bumped against the bed. He towered over her, the glint of amusement in his blue eyes a contradiction to his stern expression.

"I'm afraid I'll have to strip-search you."

He reached behind her and unfastened her bra with one quick flick, then he eased the straps from her shoulders. He didn't pull it away, though, so she drew in a deep breath and dropped it to the floor. His hot gaze dropped to her naked breasts and her nipples swelled in response. His big hands cupped her and she felt faint with desire.

With one hand on her shoulder, he pressed her to a sitting position, then onto her back. He crouched between her knees and caressed her breasts, sending thrilling sensations dancing through her. His hands patted down her sides and over her hips, then he tucked his fingers under the elastic of her panties and drew them down and off. His hot gaze on her exposed folds made her melt inside.

"Officer, are you going to put me in jail?" She gazed up at him innocently.

He smiled. "Not if you cooperate."

She rested her hand on his chest and drifted downward, loving the feel of his hard muscles beneath her fingertips. "Of course, Officer. I'll do anything you want."

He stood up and she continued gliding down his stomach, then over the big bulge straining at his boxers. He groaned as she reached inside and wrapped her fingers around his thick, hot flesh. She drew out his cock and gazed at it. He was so big, and hard as marble. She leaned forward and licked the mushroom-shaped crown, to his groan of appreciation.

"Do you like that, Officer?"

"Oh, yeah."

She wrapped her lips around him, swallowing the crown into her mouth. She drew him in deeper, then eased back. At the same time, she tucked her hands under his balls and fondled them.

"Stop, ma'am. I have other business to attend to first."

Lindsay gazed up at him in surprise, allowing his cock to slip from her lips. He knelt down and cupped her breast, then licked her hard nipple. As she gazed down, watching his head switch between her nipples, all she could see was the top of his blue cap. Then he sucked her nipple and her head fell back as she moaned. He switched and sucked the other nipple, then kissed down her stomach. He pressed her thighs wide, then he leaned toward her folds. The brim of his hat pressed on her stomach and the hat toppled from his head onto her ribs. His mouth covered her folds, then his tongue flicked inside her, sending pleasure quivering through her. She grabbed the hat, which was blocking her view, and tossed it aside.

He lifted her legs and rested them over his shoulders, giving him better access. He drove his tongue deep into her, then licked the length of her slit. With his thumbs, he parted the petals of flesh and licked the delicate button within.

"Oh, yes."

As he licked, he glided two fingers inside her and stroked her passage. She arched against him, wanting more. His fingers slid into her again and again as his tongue cajoled her sensitive nub. She grasped his head, forking her fingers through his short hair, holding him close to her. Suddenly, the rising pleasure burst through her and she cried out in orgasm.

He lifted his head and smiled at her.

She opened her arms to him. "Oh, God, please fuck me."

He wrapped his hands around her waist and guided her farther onto the bed, then grabbed a condom from his bedside table. He rolled it on, then prowled over her. She licked her lips at the sight of him grasping his big cock and pressing it to her folds. It was hard and hot as it pushed against her. Her slick flesh offered no resistance as it parted to allow him entry.

He drove forward and she gasped.

"You feel so good around me." He captured her lips, his tongue diving into her.

When he released her, she sucked in air as she stared up at him. She couldn't believe this sexy police officer had his cock deep inside her. She arched against him, pushing him deeper still, and he groaned.

He smiled and nuzzled her neck. "You are cooperative, aren't you?"

Then he drew back and drove deep again. His big cock stroked her insides as he glided in and out, pumping into her with powerful thrusts. She clung to his shoulders and wrapped her legs around his hips, opening herself wider to him. His cock drove in even deeper and she gasped.

Pleasure swelled higher with every thrust. She moaned at the exquisite sensations, teetering on the edge of the abyss. Then he thrust faster and she moaned as an orgasm blasted through her. She held on as he rode her to heaven, groaning his own release.

She collapsed on the bed and smiled up at him. "That was spectacular."

He smiled. "I aim to please."

He kissed her, then drew her close to his body. She rested her head against his chest, soothed by the sound of his heartbeat against her ear. She sighed, delighted at how the evening had turned out, and soon felt herself dozing off.

———

When Erik awoke, it was still dark outside. Lindsay's soft body was still pressed close to him. Her face snuggled in the crook of his neck. Her warm breath caressed his skin as she slept. Her round breasts nestled against his naked chest. His cock hardened at the knowledge he could just ease forward and slide into her hot opening.

Damn it, he'd barely met the woman, but ever since he'd seen her in the elevator he'd wanted her with an intensity he'd never known before. Her first touch had flooded him with images of her naked body and him gliding into her with powerful thrusts.

Lindsay murmured in her sleep, then rolled onto her other side, but moved back against him, until her delightful ass pressed against his groin. His cock twitched and his hormones urged him to do what he would have loved to do then. To slide his cock into her from behind.

She murmured in her sleep again, then wriggled her soft ass against him. Her back arched, pushing her harder against him.

"Lindsay," he murmured against her ear. "Are you awake?"

Oh, God, please be awake.

She shifted, pressing against his now painfully hard erection. "Mmm. A little." Her sweet, sleep-hoarsened voice set his body tingling.

Her hand slid back over his hip and stroked the side of his buttocks. "I can tell you're awake, too."

He grasped her hips and pulled her tight against him,

crushing her sweet ass against the length of his shaft. "I'm *very* awake."

She giggled softly. "I can tell." She arched her back again, which angled her bottom against him. "So are you going to do something about it?"

At her blatant invitation, he rolled on a condom and pressed his cock to her slick folds, then pushed forward. As her soft, hot flesh surrounded him, he groaned. She felt incredible. Then she tightened, squeezing his cock, and wild, heady sensations swirled through him.

"Damn, woman, you'll make me come before we even get started."

She laughed, then squeezed again. He drew back and plunged forward again, his hands still grasping her hips. As he thrust into her, her breathing became erratic and lovely little murmurs of pleasure escaped her lips. He nuzzled her neck and she moaned.

"Erik, that"—she moaned—"feels so good. Ahhh."

He thrust again and she continued to moan, her flesh tightening around him. He kept thrusting.

"Oh, God, I'm going to . . ." Her head fell back against his shoulder as she wailed.

His balls tightened and red-hot pleasure catapulted through him as he exploded in orgasm. His arm, tight around her, held her close as he shuddered against her.

He cuddled her close as they both caught their breath. Damn it, this was dangerous to his sanity. He didn't want to remember what it was like to have a woman in his bed like this. To have a woman in his life.

Every woman he loved had caused him pain and he didn't want to hurt like that again. As long as he remembered that, everything would be fine.

What he really wanted was to convince her to follow her desire and actually go ahead with the fantasy weekend with the three of them. This was always meant to be a weekend fling, no more.

Erik opened his eyes to a view of Lindsay facing him on the pillow, her blue eyes watching him.

"Uh, good morning."

She smiled. "Morning."

He drew her in for a kiss. The feel of her warm, naked body pressed against him made him long to glide into her sweet, hot depths again.

Their lips parted and she sighed softly.

"I guess the other guys are up," she said.

"Did you hear them?" Erik was surprised since his bedroom was farther down the hall than theirs and the guys were usually pretty careful not to disturb anyone still sleeping.

"No, but I can smell the coffee"—she raised her nose a little and sniffed—"and bacon."

He smiled. "Travis is probably cooking a big breakfast for all of us."

Ever since they moved in together, Travis had taken on as many domestic tasks as he could. He was uncomfortable with the fact that this penthouse was more expensive than he could afford if he were to pay a third of the rent. Erik owned the penthouse now and wouldn't think of taking rent from either Travis or Connor, but Travis had trouble being dependent on anyone, so he tried to make up for it in any way he could. Like cooking and cleaning.

"So we'll be eating with them?"

"Does that make you uncomfortable?"

She shrugged. "I thought it might be a little tense with Travis."

"You don't need to worry about what happened yesterday. I'm sure Connor explained the whole thing to him. And everything was fine when they joined us at the bar last night."

"Sure, but that's not the same as all of us sitting around a kitchen table together."

He kissed her cheek. "Really, it's not a problem. And they're both really great guys."

She gazed at him. "Why did Travis think that, anyway? That I'd judge him."

"Well, Travis has had it kind of rough. When he was seventeen, his father found out Travis was interested in guys and he beat him, then threw him out of the house. Clearly he wasn't the most understanding of fathers. Travis has been on his own ever since."

"That's terrible."

Erik nodded. "He took on a part-time job and finished high school, then worked his way through college. But you can see why he'd be predisposed to think that

47

others won't accept him or his way of life. Even his mother didn't stand up for him and I think that's what hurt him the most."

She frowned. "Now I feel so bad."

"Why? You didn't do anything wrong."

"I know but the whole misunderstanding triggered those feelings in him."

He pulled her close and nuzzled her neck. "I know one way you can make it up to him." He nibbled her earlobe. "Stay for the weekend."

"But he probably doesn't even like me."

Erik grinned. "I'm sure he'll like you if you have sex with him."

Her eyes widened. "Erik!"

"I'm kidding." He chuckled. "I'm sure he already likes you."

He rolled her onto her back and leaned over to press his lips to the base of her neck. He could feel her pulse, and it seemed to quicken as he slowly drew the covers down.

"I know Connor likes you, too." He gazed down at her naked breasts, watching the nipples pucker.

"Really?' she said a little breathlessly.

"He's laid-back and easy to get along with, but speaks his mind." He stroked his finger over the swell of her breast, loving the feel of her body trembling beneath him. "Most people don't realize how sensitive and insightful he is."

He cupped her breast and ran his thumb over her

nipple. It was hard and she drew in a little breath as he stroked it.

"Do you really want to give up this opportunity to experience a wild and sexy weekend with three hot guys?" He nuzzled her neck. "All of whom would adore you and make your every fantasy come true?"

"I don't think I could do it," she said breathlessly. "It's crazy enough that I spent the night with you. But the thought of being with three guys . . ."

"Can you honestly tell me you're not tempted?" He rolled onto his side and cupped her other breast, so he had one soft mound in each hand. "Having all of us touch you. Stroke you." He knew she couldn't. He kneaded her breasts, loving the feel of her hard nubs pressed into his palms. "Imagine last night . . . times three."

"Oh, God." She arched against him, pressing tighter into his hands.

Even though his cock was swollen hard and he would love to glide into her right now, he drew away.

She gazed at him uncertainly and he smiled.

"Just think about it." He kissed her cheek again. "I'm going to take a shower."

Lindsay couldn't believe she was actually thinking about it. Three hot guys, all devoted to making her sexual fantasies come to life. Judging from her time with Erik last night, if the other guys were anything like him, she'd have the time of her life.

Still, it just seemed too decadent. And what if she liked it?

A few moments later, Erik walked into the bedroom from the en suite bathroom, towel drying his short hair. Her gaze glided over his magnificent, naked body. His cock still stood at attention, and she'd love to grab hold of it and glide her lips over it.

He smiled as he tossed the towel onto the dresser. He opened a drawer and grabbed a clean pair of boxers, then pulled them on, hiding his big cock. He sat down on the bed beside her and tilted his head.

"I assume you're still thinking about it. You don't have to answer now. We could all spend some time together out by the pool and see if you get comfortable with the idea. Then we could ease into it."

"How exactly do I ease into having sex with three men?"

He smiled. "I'm sure we can figure that out. And you can set whatever limits you want and we'll follow them." He kissed her, then stroked her hair from her face. "Either way, you'll come and join us for breakfast, right?"

"Sure, I'll just shower first."

"Okay, good."

He leaned in and kissed her, his lips warm and insistent on hers. She wrapped her arms around his neck and drew him closer, lingering over the kiss.

Finally, he drew away. "If you keep doing that, I'll wind up back in bed with you."

She grinned. "You say that as if it's a bad thing."

"In this case, I think leaving you wanting more is a good thing." With that, he stood up and headed to the door.

Erik walked down the hall to the kitchen.

"Hey, want some eggs?" Travis stood at the stove and scooped two fried eggs from the frying pan and placed them on the plate Connor held.

"Sure." Erik didn't need to tell Travis how he liked his eggs. He knew. Over easy, still soft inside.

He watched Travis crack the shells and drop the eggs into the pan. The clear part of the egg started turning white immediately. Toast popped up from the toaster and Connor placed the four slices onto a cutting board, buttered them, sliced them in half, and divided them between two plates. He handed one plate to Erik.

These two men were his friends. His family. And his lovers. The pain of loss that being with Lindsay last night had revived in him eased a little.

I don't need a woman in my life. I have everything I need right here.

Connor opened the bag of bread. "Travis, two or three slices of toast today?"

"Make four. I'll eat what Lindsay doesn't." Travis glanced at Erik. "Is she up yet?"

"She's in the shower."

Erik took the coffee Connor handed him—with one cream and two sugars—and took a sip.

"I'll put four on anyway." Connor winked at Erik. "So you got lucky last night."

Erik grinned. "Well, sure. I've got the biggest cock. What did you expect?"

Connor chuckled. "Yeah?" With a grin on his face, he stroked Erik's crotch. "Prove it."

Erik's cock immediately started to harden.

"Break it up, boys. I don't want breakfast to get cold." Travis placed the eggs on a plate and set them on the counter, then broke open two more into a bowl and mixed them. "Mine will be ready in a minute."

"Yes, dear." But Connor gave Erik's cock a little squeeze before he drew his hand away and headed for the table.

"Thanks. How am I going to enjoy my breakfast with a hard-on?"

"Well, just sit down and maybe someone will take care of that for you." Connor stroked the bulge growing in his own boxers. "Mine, too." He glanced at Travis, who still stood by the stove. "What do you think, Travis?"

Travis poured the blended eggs into the hot pan. "So I have all the wifely duties this morning."

"Good morning."

Erik glanced around at the sound of Lindsay's voice. She looked radiant standing in the doorway, the morning light glittering on her golden hair, casting a halo around her face. And sexy wearing a body-hugging camisole and denim shorts.

How much had she heard of their conversation and

what did she think of the sexual interplay between Connor, Travis, and himself?

"Morning, doll. Join us for breakfast." Connor sat down. "There's coffee on and toast will be up in a minute. Travis is being chef this morning, so just tell him how you want your eggs."

She wandered across the room to the stove and peered around Travis into the pan. "Scrambled are fine for me."

"Are you sure?" Travis picked up two more eggs. "I can make whatever style you want."

"Sure. I don't mind having what you're having. That way we both get hot eggs."

Travis added two more eggs to the bowl, mixed them, and added them to the eggs already cooking in the pan. The toast popped up and Lindsay buttered it and put it on a plate.

"Oh, and since Travis is doing all the wifely duties this morning"—she said as she walked to the table with a definite sway to her hips, her lips turning up in an impish smile—"I could take care of that other matter, if you'd like." She sat down and glanced at Travis. "For all three of you."

Five

Shock and delight swelled through Erik at her words. So she had decided to give this a try. And she was going to jump right in.

The thought of her hand stroking his cock, then her lips surrounding it and moving over it, taking it into her warm mouth, sent heat surging through him. And then watching her with Connor and Travis . . . God, he could hardly wait.

Connor grinned broadly. "That suits me fine."

Travis arrived at the table with two plates of eggs, and a rock-hard cock straining at his boxers. He placed one plate in front of Lindsay and sat down beside her.

"After breakfast." She picked up a piece of toast and took a bite.

Ah, damn. Now he really would have to suffer a boner during his whole breakfast. Did she not realize with that announcement, all three men would clean their plates in record time?

"So what do you do for a living?" She took a sip of her coffee, then a small bite of her eggs, and chewed delicately.

Erik couldn't decide if she was eating slower than usual to keep them waiting, or if the boost of adrenaline only made it seem that way.

Travis swallowed, then washed his food down with some coffee. "Well, Connor and I just started our own business."

"Really?" She pushed her fork through a chunk of egg on her plate. "What kind of business?"

"We're developing game apps." Connor shrugged. "It's fun and we have some great ideas."

"So you're doing that part-time?"

Connor chuckled. "No, we left our jobs two weeks ago. We're taking some time off to get settled in here and get an office set up in one of the bedrooms, then we'll jump in with both feet."

"Wow, that's a big step," she said. "Quitting your jobs for a start-up."

"We're lucky," Travis replied. "We found an investor who believes in us."

Lindsay looked skeptical. And why shouldn't she? Start-ups were a risky business and she had no idea that Erik had just come into a huge inheritance from his father. Erik loved his job and wouldn't think of leaving it, but it gave him great joy to be able to make Travis and Connor's dream come true.

They hated the nine-to-five routine, and the two of them had dreamed of starting a software gaming company since they were in college. They always had a list of great ideas, but never had the time to go anywhere with them. Now all that had changed.

"And as you saw yesterday," Travis said, "Erik's a cop."

Her gaze shifted to Erik and he could see a glimmer in her blue-gray eyes. A wave of desire washed through him, complete with images of him snapping handcuffs around her wrists, then turning her around and searching her, his hands roving over her quivering body, stroking and squeezing. The thought of him in uniform definitely turned her on. Another image wafted through him, of her kneeling in front of him, then lifting her handcuffed hands to unzip his pants. His hormones went into a spin and his cock twitched.

"We'd ask you what you do," Connor said with a grin, "but right now I think we'd all rather you eat than talk."

Lindsay glanced around and realized all three men had finished their food. They were waiting for her to fulfill her promise.

Her cheeks flushed a little at her brazenness, but when she'd overheard their conversation as she'd walked into the kitchen, it seemed like a perfect way to ease into the activities of the weekend. Erik had been right when he'd pointed out that an opportunity like this didn't come along all the time. Here were three incredibly sexy men, all wanting her. And the thought of being with them sent her hormones into a tailspin.

It had been fabulous with Erik last night, and it was possible that if they got more serious, he wouldn't want to share her with his friends. But he was all right with it now and . . . even though it was wild and crazy, she'd love to experience this fantasy.

She sipped her coffee, then began to eat faster. The whole time she ate, she was intensely aware of the three sexy males sitting at the table with her, their naked male chests, broad and muscular, on display. They all seemed to believe in a casual breakfast, wearing just their boxers and, although those boxers were hidden by the tabletop, she was pretty sure they were filled with long, hard cocks right now.

Lindsay finished her last bite of egg and set down her cutlery, then glanced around at the men's expectant faces. Time to put them out of their misery.

"Okay, time for dessert." She slipped under the wooden table and glanced around at the three pairs of knees. Sure enough, she could see the outline of large bulges in all their boxers.

She crouched in front of Travis. He'd done all the work cooking breakfast, so he deserved to be first. God, could she really do this? Give oral sex to these men she hardly knew?

Her insides quivered at the illicit nature of what she was about to do. Why not? She was an adult and these three sexy men were not only gorgeous, but they made her feel cared for and respected. There was nothing wrong with allowing a decadent fantasy to come to life.

The cotton of Travis' boxers stretched over his raging erection. She stroked it and the hard flesh twitched under her hand. Excitement skittered down her spine as she glided her fingers down his length, then she leaned forward and kissed the softly furred flesh above his navel. She tucked her hand inside the opening and wrapped her fingers around his hot, hard flesh.

Oh, God, I can't believe I'm actually doing this!

But it helped being under the table, where she couldn't see their faces. And they couldn't see her. She drew him out and admired the big, mushroom-shaped head.

She licked the tip, teasing the little hole, then swirled downward in a spiral. The tip of her tongue circled under the corona and she licked around and around. She turned her head sideways and nibbled along his hot length with her lips, toward his body, then back to the top again. When she reached the corona, she glided over the top and swallowed it into her mouth.

As she licked and nibbled his cock-head, she reached out and stroked over Connor's boxers. He tugged his cock out and she wrapped her hand around his thick shaft and stroked up and down. Then she dove down on Travis, his big cock filling her throat.

Erik could tell by the look on Travis' face that Lindsay was giving him some very close attention. Travis sucked in a breath and Erik knew she must have swallowed him deep. By Connor's increased breathing, she must be stroking him, too.

Erik watched his two friends' faces contort in pleasure and he imagined the feel of her mouth covering him. Sucking him.

He couldn't help squeezing his cloth-covered bulge as Travis groaned, his body shifting up and down, probably as his cock glided in and out of Lindsay's mouth.

A moment later, Erik felt Lindsay's hand brush his aside, then stroke over his boxers. Her fingers pushed under the fabric and wrapped around his aching cock. She drew him out and began to stroke, her fingers around him firmly.

Connor arched in his chair. "Fuck, doll, that's great." His hand disappeared under the table, probably to stroke her head.

Erik sucked in a breath as Lindsay's hand stroked Erik's cock with enthusiasm.

Then he felt her body move against his knees and . . . oh, God, her tongue lapped across the tip of his cock. He slumped back in his chair, giving himself over to her ministrations. She licked around his cock-head, then dipped her tongue under the corona and glided around. Pleasure shimmered through him at her delicate touch. Then her hand tightened around him and she stroked again, as her mouth wrapped around his cock-head, enveloping it in warmth.

He had to touch her. He slid his hand over the crown of her head, forking his fingers through her long, silky hair. Her lips glided downward. His cock filled her mouth, then slid deep into her throat. He thought he'd died and gone to heaven. His cock felt as if it would burst.

Her fingers teased his balls, then she cradled them in her palm. As her mouth moved up and down his hot shaft, his body quivered with pleasure. Waves of heat washed through him, building to blissful sensations. She squeezed him in her mouth, the hand around his cock tightening at the same time and stroking rapidly.

"Oh, God, sweetheart."

Then she released his cock and ducked out from under the table. She peered around at them uncertainly.

"That was great," said Travis.

Connor grinned. "Definitely."

Erik had a desperate need to be close to her, so he stood up and tugged her into his arms, then kissed her passionately, driving his tongue deep into her mouth. When he released her, she was breathless, her eyes glazed with need, but to his surprise, she smiled and drew away.

"So it's your turn now," Erik said, imagining his hard flesh sinking into her.

"No. I think that earned me the right to avoid the

dishes, so you three should do them while I go sit by the pool." Her smile turned impish. "Just don't watch me out the window." She giggled as she opened the patio door and stepped into the sunshine.

Six

Lindsay waltzed across the patio, wondering where she'd found this wonderful brazenness that allowed her to give three men oral sex and leave them hard as rocks, and then to do what she intended to do now.

She shed her shirt as she walked. A surreptitious glance at the kitchen window showed her the guys were indeed watching her. She dropped her shorts to the ground, then ignoring the flash of embarrassment at the thought of Connor and Travis seeing her naked for the first time, she quickly stripped off her bra and panties, and lay down on one of the cushioned lounge chairs.

God, she was turned on after having those three big cocks in her mouth. At the memory of hot, hard flesh gliding into her mouth, her already slick core demanded her attention. But first, she slid her hand over her breast and stroked it, then tweaked her hard nipple. Her other hand covered her other breast and she squeezed lightly.

The sun caressed her body with warmth and she sighed happily. She slid a hand down her stomach, past the navel, to the slick folds, then dipped inside, burying two fingers into the dampness.

She was so primed, especially after Erik teasing her in the bedroom and purposefully leaving her needy. She squeezed and arched against her hand. She glided her fingers out again and stroked over her clit. Oh, it felt so good. She flicked over it and . . . oh, God, she hadn't realized she was so close. As she flicked again, pleasure washed over her in waves. Tossing her head back against the cushion, she arched and moaned against her hand. She imagined Erik's mouth covering her, his tongue lapping across her sensitive clit.

She catapulted to orgasm, moaning and arching. Riding the wave of bliss. Then she fell back against the chair, sucking in air.

Erik watched Lindsay finger-fucking herself on the deck and his cock swelled to full attention. He couldn't help grabbing his cock and stroking at the erotic sight of her moaning and arching her beautiful, naked body.

Finally, she fell back against the chair, spent.

He glanced around and both his friends were also stroking their hard cocks.

"Well, it looks like she's going to enjoy the sun for a while," Travis said. "How about we give each other a hand?"

Connor followed Travis into the living room and Erik followed right behind them. As soon as Erik sank into the armchair, Travis crouched in front of him and wrapped his hand around Erik's cock. The firm, strong grip excited him, but after a few strokes, he stopped him.

"I want to watch you two." Erik glanced from Travis to Connor.

Connor grabbed Travis by the shoulders and tumbled him onto his back on the carpeted floor, then tossed his knees over Travis' legs, pinning him between his legs. Then he grabbed Travis' cock. Fascinated, Erik watched the bulbous purple head glide in and out of view as Connor stroked.

The sun beat down on Lindsay as she lay naked. She had satisfied her immediate need, but she still wanted more. She glanced at the window but the men were no longer watching her. Not that she thought they would once she'd finished. She pushed herself to her feet and rolled her clothes into a bundle, then walked to the patio door. As she reached for the handle, she saw Erik sitting on the couch, his tall erection clutched in his hand, and Connor on the floor, sitting on Travis as he stroked the man's long cock.

Oh, God, it was such an exciting sight. Her breathing stopped as Connor leaned forward and wrapped his lips around Travis' big purple cock-head. She quivered in excitement.

I shouldn't be watching this.

But they were doing it in the living room. A common area of the apartment. If they'd wanted privacy, they would have gone into one of the bedrooms. Still, she didn't want to open the door because it might disturb them and change the dynamic. So she stayed on the other side of the glass. She cupped her breast as she watched Connor's head bob up and down on Travis.

Erik caught sight of a movement outside. He gazed at the patio door and saw Lindsay peering in, watching Connor and Travis with wide eyes. Then he realized she was stroking her breast, and her other hand glided down her stomach and curled over her mound.

Oh, God, he had to have his cock inside her. He stood up and crossed the room. Her blue eyes widened even more as she saw him coming. He opened the door.

"Come inside and watch." He took her hand and she followed him into the room.

She glanced at Connor and Travis, but they were too busy to take notice of her. Erik watched the long cock glide in and out of Connor's mouth as he led Lindsay to the couch.

He took the clothes from her hand and dropped them on the floor, then turned her around to face the men, her naked ass pressed against his rock-hard cock.

He nuzzled her ear. "Are you as turned on as I am?"

"Oh, God, yes."

He chuckled and grabbed a condom from the drawer in the side table, then sat down. He opened the packet and rolled the condom on his erection as he watched her hungrily watch Connor and Travis. The fact it turned her on so much turned him on even more. He grasped her hips.

"Come here, sweetheart."

As she lowered onto his lap, he positioned the tip of his cock below her. When he rubbed against her slick opening, she stopped, allowing him to position himself. She lowered a little more, swallowing his cock-head in her hot opening. He groaned at the exquisite feel of her velvety, moist flesh around him. She lowered quickly, taking him deep inside her.

Lindsay's gaze remained glued to Connor repeatedly swallowing Travis' big cock, intensely aware of Erik's big cock inside her. Travis tossed his head back and moaned loudly. Lindsay squeezed Erik inside her and he groaned.

Travis sat up and turned Connor around. Connor leaned against the seat of the armchair in front of him and Travis pressed his cock-head to Connor's ass. Then he drove forward, to Connor's groan.

Erik grabbed her hips and lifted her a little, then lowered her again. She rested her hands on his knees and continued the motion, lifting herself and dropping back down, taking his cock deep. Erik's hands slid around her and covered her breasts. Travis drove into Connor again and again, while Erik toyed with her nipples, driving her insane with need.

"Oh, fuck, I'm coming." Connor arched and moaned.

Travis drove in hard, and groaned while he held Connor tight to his body, obviously following him to climax.

Lindsay realized she'd stopped moving on Erik's huge cock. Instead of continuing with her up and down movement, she swirled her hips in a circular motion, stirring his big, thick cock inside her.

His fingers found her clit and stroked the sensitive bud. He flicked a couple of times, then grasped her hips and lifted her up and down again.

"Oh, my God." Pleasure spiked through her and she squeezed Erik's big, marble-hard cock as it drove into her. "Oh, faster," she pleaded.

He lifted her faster. Soon, he began to groan and blissful sensations swamped her senses.

"Oh, God, I'm coming." She gasped. "You're . . . ahhh . . . making me." She moaned. "Come."

The orgasm tore through her like a flash storm, blasting all her senses with intense pleasure. She continued to moan as the pleasure swept through her.

As Lindsay rested against Erik's chest, she suddenly realized she was totally naked in front of three equally naked men. She eased away from Erik and grabbed her bra from the floor, then glanced around, looking for her undies.

"Looking for this?" Connor grinned as he held out his hand, her skimpy thong dangling from his outstretched finger.

"Yes, thank you." Her cheeks burned red. She sounded ridiculously prim and proper after what had just happened. For heaven's sake, she'd gotten super aroused while watching Connor and Travis fuck each other silly, then she'd climbed aboard Erik for the ride of her life.

God, she'd never been so uninhibited. But now she was just embarrassed.

She took the fabric dangling from his finger and turned her back to the men while she pulled on the undies, then quickly slid into the bra and fastened it snugly.

When she turned around, the men were pulling on their boxers. She quickly located her shorts and camisole and pulled them on, too. Erik smiled warmly at her, and not one of the men smirked at her sudden fit of self-consciousness, though she suspected Connor had to work hard at suppressing the grin he'd been sporting only moments before.

"I have to confess," Erik said, "that we never did get those dishes done."

"I think it's only fair that Erik and I clean up after breakfast," Connor said, "while you and Travis take a break by the pool. After all, Travis cooked breakfast and you"—he winked—"gave us all a treat."

Her cheeks heated even more, but then she was being shooed out the door.

"I can help with the dishes," Travis said and Lindsay

wondered if it was because he didn't want to be alone with her.

"No way," Connor said.

The patio door slid closed behind her and Travis, and she glanced at him. He shrugged and headed for the pool.

"Do you want to go for a swim?" he asked.

Cooling off wouldn't be a bad idea. She nodded. He strode to the diving board and dove in, his exquisite male body streamlined as it sliced through the water. She walked to the side of the pool and dove in from there. They both swam in silence for a while, then she pulled herself from the water and sat on the side of the deep end, dangling her legs in. A moment later, Travis pulled himself from the water, droplets streaming from his body like glittering diamonds in the bright sunlight. He sat on the side and pushed his long, dark brown hair back from his eyes. Because of the curved edge of the pool they were angled toward each other.

"I'm curious about something."

Lindsay glanced up at his words. He stared at her intently.

"What's that?" she asked.

"What did you think about what just happened?"

She knew he didn't mean in the pool. Memories of Erik's hard cock inside her while she watched Connor and Travis skittered through her brain. Her cheeks flushed again and she stammered, "I guess I'm a little uncomfortable about it."

His expression tightened. "So you don't approve of Connor and me together?"

Her gaze darted to his. The warmth in his brown eyes had diminished and his lips were a taut line. Oh, damn. She'd done it again.

"No, that's not what I meant. I'm just a little self-conscious"—her gaze dropped to her hands—"well, a lot self-conscious about my behavior."

"Lindsay."

She raised her gaze to his again.

"You don't need to be self-conscious. None of us will judge you, except in the most positive way. It's great that you opened up and allowed yourself to go with what you felt."

She nodded at his encouragement. "Thanks. And about you and Connor, it was really sexy watching the two of you."

He nodded. "So you find it a turn-on."

"Well, yeah. You're both so sexy and so open with each other."

"And what if Erik got involved, too?"

Her body tingled as goose bumps quivered along her arms. "That would be . . . *really* sexy." That much testosterone involved in groping, sweaty, masculine sex would take her breath away.

His gaze met hers, but she sensed he'd hoped for more. It being a turn-on for her wasn't enough.

"You know, Travis, it's not just that it's really sexy

watching you. I think it's wonderful that you are all so comfortable with your sexuality and that you are comfortable loving who you want to love, not bound by society's norms."

"You think I'm in love with Connor?"

"Oh, I wasn't saying you have to be in love with someone to have sex with them." Oh, no, had she offended him again? "I just mean, you seem to be open to being with whomever you have feelings for and I assume you're open to falling in love and—"

He held up his hand, his lips quirking up in an amused smile. "It's okay, Lindsay. The relationship between me and Connor . . . and Erik, for that matter . . . is complicated. I don't expect you to understand it. Hell, we don't really understand it fully ourselves." As he stared at her, his amused expression turned serious again. "So you're really saying you're okay with me loving Connor—another man—and possibly Erik, and still wanting to have sex with you? You don't see anything wrong with all of us being free and open about our sexuality while still having a loving relationship with each other?"

She shrugged. "Of course not. As long as you're all okay with it, why would I have a problem with it? I actually think it's really great."

A smile spread across his face again, and this time warmth lit his eyes. He stood up and stepped toward her, then offered his hand.

"You're a very special woman, Lindsay."

She took his hand and he drew her to her feet, then

into his arms. With his hard body pressed the length of hers, his arms around her in a warm embrace, she expected her libido to kick in, but instead she felt . . . warm and accepted. And loved. Her arms slid around him and she held him close. Clearly, they weren't *in love,* but there was a loving glow of shared appreciation in that hug. And something more.

She sensed he needed this more than he'd ever admit. According to Erik, Travis had been on his own since he was seventeen and he didn't allow many people to get close. Maybe he craved the nurturing warmth of a woman.

If this were a normal, casual hug, it would end about now, but when she started to release him, he tightened his arms around her, and her heart swelled. He was showing her a level of vulnerability that touched her deeply. She tightened her arms around him and reveled in the glow of this intimate and loving closeness.

Erik rinsed the suds from a mug and put it in the drainer.

"So it looks like she's going to stay," Connor said.

"Seems like it. We need to let her ease into things at her own pace."

Connor chuckled. "Easing into her is exactly what I want to do."

Erik glanced out the window and noticed Lindsay and Travis in an embrace, their bodies in full contact. His jaw clenched and he had to ignore the twang of jealousy rising in him.

"What's that all about?" Connor asked while peering over Erik's shoulder.

They both knew that Travis didn't bond easily with anyone and seeing him hugging Lindsay with such warmth was odd.

"I don't know. Maybe they talked about yesterday's misunderstanding and sorted things out."

"I guess."

He grinned at Connor's serious expression. "You aren't jealous, are you?"

"No. You kidding? We've all shared enough women that you know that's not going to happen."

It was true, they had. But Travis had always held back. He was enthusiastic when it came to the sex, but he wasn't big on physical contact with a woman other than that. Yet there he was, hugging Lindsay like she was a long-lost friend.

It would be good for him to open up to someone other than Erik and Connor.

Erik pushed aside the uneasy thought that there was one other woman Travis had opened up to. Becci, who had nearly torn the three of them apart.

But this wasn't the same thing.

"It's good that he's opening up to Lindsay," Erik said.

"You're right." But uncertainty showed in Connor's eyes.

Connor and Travis had been together a long time.

Longer than they'd known Erik. Could Connor be worried that Lindsay was a threat to that relationship?

He placed his hand on Connor's shoulder and smiled. "Come on. Let's go out and join them."

Travis didn't want to let her go. He didn't want this closeness to end. In Lindsay's arms, he felt nurtured and cared for in a way that was both deep and profound.

He understood that it probably had something to do with the fact he'd been rejected by his mother and that on some level he deeply craved the love of a woman, but he didn't want to analyze it. He just wanted to enjoy the comfort of her soft embrace.

He heard the patio door slide open. Damn. He released her and stepped back. Her gaze flickered over his and from the uncertainty in her eyes, he could tell the hug had affected her, too.

He glanced at his approaching friends. Erik carried two beers and Connor had a beer and a hard lemonade, which he held out to Lindsay.

"Drink?" Connor asked.

"Sure, thanks." She took the frosty bottle from his hand.

Travis took the beer Erik offered and took a swig.

Connor sent Travis a questioning gaze and he realized Connor was surprised, and maybe a little put off, at the hug. Did he feel threatened by Lindsay?

Should he?

"I'm going to change," Lindsay said.

Travis watched her as she walked to the patio door and realized he wanted to get to know her better. He wanted to spend time with her. He wanted to be *intimate* with her.

Sharing her with Connor and Erik would be exciting, but he also longed to have her to himself.

Damn, he cared deeply for Connor, but he wanted to explore what he was feeling with Lindsay. Would that hurt his relationship with Connor?

Seven

Lindsay walked to the balcony's edge and glanced over the concrete rail to the city below. It was hot out, but a warm breeze wisped across her cheeks, lifting her hair in a soft caress. The river glittered in the sunshine. She could see the green park skirting one edge, and a myriad of buildings and streets laid out below them.

She turned back to the lovely pool and walked to the teak chairs where the men had settled and joined them.

"So what do you do?" Travis asked as he swirled his beer.

"I work for a research company."

"And what do you do there?" he asked.

"I manage a system that indexes confidential documents and allows me to retrieve the physical copies when someone in the company needs them."

Connor grinned. "So you're a librarian."

"My title is Document Retrieval Manager."

"Very impressive, but I like librarian better." Connor's lips turned up in an ultra sexy grin, sending quivers down her spine. "I can just imagine you with your hair up in a bun, glasses, and wearing a bulky wool suit."

"I don't wear my hair in a bun and I don't wear glasses." Sometimes she did coil her hair back and fasten it with a clip, but that wasn't a bun. And she wore contact lenses.

"And the suit?" Travis asked.

"A lot of women wear suits to work," she said defensively.

Erik chuckled. "They're teasing you. They just like the idea of you being all prim and proper, so they can peel away the outer layer to find the sexy filling inside."

He caught her gaze and she almost gasped as images of herself dressed in a business suit, her hair in a tight bun, and thick black glasses on her face flashed through her brain . . . then Erik stepping toward her and taking off the glasses. Then unpinning her long, blonde hair so it tumbled around her shoulders. *His fingers reached for the buttons of her jacket and her heart raced as he unfastened them, one by one.*

She took a long sip of her drink, her gaze flickering away. Damn, the idea of spending a fantasy sex weekend with these men was really addling her brain.

She wanted to ask them about the invitation, and how they knew about her fantasy of being with three men, but she couldn't quite get up the nerve. Partly because she'd have to admit it was true.

"This is a great place." She wondered how they could afford such a luxurious place.

"We're lucky. A friend of ours inherited it and is letting us live here," Connor said.

"Is that the same friend who invested in your business?" she asked.

Connor's gaze flicked to Erik.

"That's right," Erik answered.

She shifted in her chair. "Does that mean he, or she, might show up?"

Erik grinned. "No one's going to walk in on us skinny-dipping in the pool, if that's what you're worried about."

"Skinny-dipping?" Travis grinned at her with a gleam in his eye. "That sounds like a great idea."

He stood up and tugged off his T-shirt, then dropped his jeans, followed quickly by his boxers. She couldn't help but gaze at his long cock as it dangled in front of him.

He raised his eyebrows. "Coming?"

"Not yet," Connor said, also gazing at Travis' big cock, "but give me time." He stood up and stripped, then followed Travis to the pool.

Lindsay watched their fine tight butts as they walked. Both dove into the water.

"So no one's going to show up unexpectedly?" she asked Erik as they watched Connor and Travis surface, sunlight glittering on their damp hair.

"That's right.

He was awfully confident about it.

It seemed odd they had a rich friend who let them

live in this apartment, but who didn't live here, too. She glanced at Erik and wondered if this mysterious friend might not be one of them.

He smiled. "So you've decided to stay and give this a try?"

She shifted in her chair. She had already taken her first steps, so why was she hesitating?

Erik watched her patiently.

This weekend was her opportunity to be wild and crazy. To indulge in her fantasy, sharing it with these wildly sexy men.

"Yes," she finally answered. Her gaze drifted to the pool as Connor pushed himself onto the side. "I'm curious, though. Why did you send me that invitation?"

"It was pretty clear on that elevator ride that you were hot for the three of us, so it seemed like it was worth a try."

"So how did you get the invitation to me? Jill must have helped you."

"And if I tell you she did, will you be mad at her?"

"Maybe a little." But she smiled, knowing that the way things were working out, she was actually happy Jill had gone along with them. It meant Jill must have mentioned her to them, otherwise how would they know she and Jill were friends?

"Even if I tell you she had no idea what was in the envelope? Connor just told her that we would love a chance to meet you, so we wanted to send you a letter from a secret admirer. She loved the idea, so she was game. She didn't let us know where you lived. You really shouldn't be mad at her."

She grinned as she leaned back in her chair. "I suppose I could be convinced to forgive her." She glanced back at the men in the pool. "So what made you think I was hot for you?"

Erik's gaze fell on Travis as he pulled himself onto the side of the pool beside Connor, his lips turning up in a grin. "You're kidding, right?" He chuckled. "You women sometimes have a double standard. I bet you wouldn't have been happy if I'd been as preoccupied with your chest as you had been with ours."

"Well, if my chest were at your eye level . . ." She shrugged, her lips curling up. His eyes glittered with amusement. "Come over here for a minute."

Her brows pressed together. "Why? "

"Just come on over."

She stood up and approached him. He turned his chair and perched forward, then took her forearms and guided her to stand in front of him. Then he stared at her breasts, which were right in front of his face.

And he stared.

She felt prickles along her spine, and her nipples hardened.

"Okay, I get it." But she didn't move away.

His hand lifted and he caressed the side of one breast. She could feel the warmth of his hand through the thin fabric of her shirt and bra.

The breath locked in her lungs, and he caressed the

other breast in the same manner, then his fingers glided under both mounds and he lifted the weight of them in his hands. She rested her hands on his shoulders, loving the feel of his rigid muscles under her fingers.

As he continued to caress her, she glanced toward the pool. Both men were at the shallow end, Connor sitting on the side of the pool and Travis in the water facing him. Travis' hand was wrapped around Connor's big cock, stroking it. He leaned forward and took Connor's cock-head into his mouth.

"It's sexy watching them, isn't it?" Erik said.

She nodded, never tearing her gaze from the erotic sight of Travis swallowing Connor's humungous erection.

Connor leaned back on his hands, his eyes closed, and arched his pelvis to Travis' mouth. He started to moan and Travis bounced up and down, Connor's long cock gliding between his lips. Erik's thumbs brushed over her sensitive nipples, sending heat thrumming through her.

The muscles along Connor's arms and shoulders strained as his face contorted in pleasure. He groaned as Travis sucked him hard, then collapsed on the deck, panting. Lindsay murmured at the erotic sensation of Erik stroking her nipples through the cloth as Travis pushed himself out of the water and sat on the deck beside Connor.

Erik shifted his chair to face the pool and guided her into his lap. She watched Travis stroke his hand over Connor's rippled abs. Erik cupped her breasts as he held her close. Connor sat up and grabbed Travis' cock and stroked.

Erik's thumbs gliding over her nipples sent sparks careening through her.

Connor's mouth covered Travis' cock, then the big shaft disappeared inside him. She arched back against Erik. His hand skimmed over her ribs toward her hip, then stroked over the crotch of her shorts. Oh, God, she wanted to feel his fingers against her opening. He stroked more firmly and she could feel the slickness between her legs.

"Are you wet?" He murmured the question against her ear, his breath stirring wisps of hair at her temple.

She nodded and tucked her hand between them to graze the tip of his hard bulge. "And you're hard as a rock."

He chuckled. "What do you expect with your sexy body against me like this?"

"And those two hard bodies over there getting it on." She watched Connor bob up and down on Travis, the hard shaft of flesh filling Connor's mouth each time.

"Too true." He flicked her nipple, eliciting a gasp from her.

Her eyelids fell closed as he squeezed both nipples through the cloth. Her head fell back against his chest and she arched her pelvis. He glided one hand down her ribs and stroked her aching opening again. Damn, there was too much cloth in the way.

"Hey, that's a fucking sexy show."

At Connor's voice, she opened her eyes. He stood in front of her, naked and dripping wet, Travis beside him. Both their cocks were fully erect.

God, she had three hunky men panting over her, ready and willing to grant her every sexual whim.

Her gaze ran over their bulging erections and excitement swelled through her. She'd made her decision to give herself this weekend to be wild and crazy. To indulge her wickedest fantasies with these wildly sexy men.

But she didn't know how to get started. She felt awkward and unsure of herself.

As if sensing her uncertainty, Erik tipped her face toward him, then his lips meshed with hers.

Heat flashed through her and her inner passage clenched. She longed for his cock to be inside her, within the grip of her tightly squeezing internal muscles. His tongue glided along the seam of her mouth and she opened, then her tongue dodged out to meet his. They tangled together, and she twisted around in his lap. His hand glided up her ribs and he cupped her breast again. Her fingers glided through his short hair and she murmured as sweet yearning pulsed through her.

When he released her mouth, she drew in a deep breath, then grabbed the hem of her camisole and tugged it over her head. Then she reached behind her and unfastened her bra and let the straps slide from her shoulders. All she had to do was peel it away and they would see her naked breasts and her swollen nipples. But she hesitated, suddenly feeling too brash.

Erik nuzzled her neck, sending tingles along her spine, then he trailed one fingertip along the lacy edge of her bra, over her tingling flesh. He tucked an index finger under each strap and gazed at her. Waiting. She nodded and he peeled the bra from her breasts. His gaze dropped to her rigid nipples.

He lifted her from his lap and settled her on the lounge chair beside them.

"You look really cold." He kissed her shoulder, then glided downward.

As his lips covered her left nipple, she gasped. His hot mouth felt incredible on her.

Immediately, Travis stepped forward. "I would love to touch you."

Oh, God, this was it. The first step to letting all three of them make love to her.

She gazed up at his chocolate-brown eyes, filled with need, and nodded.

He dropped in front of her and dragged his fingertip over her swollen nipple. She moaned softly at his gentle touch. He smiled and leaned forward to lick her nub, then draw it into his mouth. Both Erik and Travis licked and sucked and she moaned at the intense sensations throbbing through her. Her head fell back and she gazed at Connor, standing a few feet away, his hard cock in his hand. She licked her lips as she watched him. He smiled and stepped toward her.

Both men at her breasts began to suck and she moaned again. She longed to touch Connor's marble-hard cock, so she wrapped her hand around it. He stepped closer and she drew it to her mouth, then pressed the hot tip to her lips. Someone's hand glided down her leg to her knee, then stroked up again, along her inner thigh. Lindsay opened her mouth and swirled her tongue over Connor's cock-head, then she wrapped her lips around his shaft as he pushed inside.

Someone unfastened her shorts and pushed them down to her ankles. She kicked them away. The fingers gliding up her thigh found her panties and stroked over her crotch. Lightly. She arched against the fingers, wanting more. They stroked more firmly, then glided along her slit. She squeezed Connor's cock in her mouth. When more fingers glided to her panties, then slid underneath and dipped into her moistness, she sucked on the big cock in her mouth, her hand stroking its length.

"Sweet thing," Travis said, "you are so frigging wet."

She felt hands tug at the elastic of her panties and she lifted her butt so they could peel them away. The men grasped her thighs and drew her forward. Connor pushed a little deeper into her mouth and she squeezed him with her lips and her hand.

She almost jumped when she felt lips nuzzle her navel, then move downward. When the mouth nuzzled her folds and a tongue pushed against her clit, she moaned, Connor's penis slipping from her mouth. She tried to draw it back in, but he moved away.

"It's okay, doll. I'd rather watch you come."

"Oh, God." She arched her pelvis upward, toward the hungry mouth, as her gaze fell to her lap. It was Erik feasting on her.

Travis winked at her, then her eyes fell closed as Erik

sucked on her clit. Pleasure trembled through her. His fingers stroked along her slit, then two glided inside her. She squeezed them tightly, wishing it was a cock in there. But then he lapped at her clit again, and sucked. Joyful sensations blossomed within her, and an orgasm shuddered through her.

She realized she was holding his head firmly against her, her fingers gliding through his short-cropped hair. She released him, gazing at him with wide eyes. She couldn't believe this sexy police officer, and his roommates, were making love to her.

Erik stood up, then took Lindsay's hand and drew her to her feet. He grabbed a condom from the bowl on the table. They'd put a bowl of colorful condoms out here and in the living room so they'd be handy over the weekend. He opened the packet and rolled it on, then walked toward her, anxious to feel her soft body against him. To feel her heat surrounding his hard, aching shaft. She watched him, her sweet blue eyes glazed and locked on his twitching erection.

He wrapped his arms around her and pulled her tightly to him, almost groaning at the feel of her soft breasts crushed against his chest, her bead-hard nipples pressing into him. He couldn't help himself. He devoured her mouth, thrusting his tongue into her sweetness. Tasting her. Groaning as she sucked on his tongue, drawing it even deeper into her warmth.

When he released her mouth, she gazed at him with longing.

"Please fuck me, Officer."

Oh, God, he couldn't have stopped himself if he'd wanted to. He backed her up to the lounge chair, then grabbed the long, flat cushion and threw it on the deck, then eased her onto the soft surface. He positioned himself over her and pressed his cock against her slick opening.

"Do it," she said, gazing into his eyes. "Fill me with every inch of you."

Never losing eye contact, he drove forward, filling her with one thrust. She moaned.

God, she felt so sweet around him. Slick and hot. Soft.

He drew back, then drove forward again. Her eyes glazed.

"You like that?" he asked as he drove into her again.

"Oh, yes."

Her muscles tightened around him and he groaned.

He nuzzled her neck, then captured her gaze again. Focusing on her eyes, he thrust again and again. She began to gasp, her body tightening. She whimpered, then her eyes widened and she began to moan.

My God, she's beautiful when she comes.

His heart throbbed and then white-hot pleasure jolted through him. He groaned, an echo to her long, intense wail of pleasure. She clung to his shoulders, wailing on and on, her body arching against him.

Then she went limp.

He relaxed against her, resting on his elbows and knees so he wouldn't crush her under his weight. Her eyes were closed.

"I think she fell asleep," Travis said as they all stared at her unconscious body. "Funny, she didn't seem bored a minute ago."

Eight

"Very funny. She's not sleeping. She passed out," Connor said. "That happens sometimes when the fucking is really intense."

"I know. They call it *la petite mort*." Travis knelt at her side and stroked her hand. "The little death."

Erik scooped her up and carried her across the deck, his chest tightening in concern. Travis opened the patio door and Erik carried her inside and down the hall to the master bedroom. Connor got the door this time, then Erik carried her to the king-sized bed.

Lindsay felt a solid chest against her face and strong arms under her back and legs. Her body jostled as someone carried her.

"Grab the covers." It was Erik's voice.

Her eyelids flicked open. What was going on?

Erik was carrying her in his arms. Memories of him kissing her, then driving that incredible cock of his into her, sent her heart racing. He'd taken her to such heights of pleasure, she'd blacked out.

Travis pulled back the covers on the bed and Erik set her down, the soft mattress compressing beneath her, then he covered her with the sheet.

"I'll get a glass of water. You two stay with her." Erik hurried away.

Travis noticed her eyes were open. "Hey, are you okay?"

"Yes, I'm fine." She smiled to reassure them.

"Actually"—Connor's gaze locked on her nipples making a sharp outline through the sheet—"you look a little cold. How about I warm you up?" He climbed into the bed behind her and snuggled her close to his body.

Travis climbed in the other side of the bed and smiled from the pillow beside hers.

"You all look pretty comfortable," Erik said as he returned with a glass of water in his hand. "Are you . . . okay?" He looked so serious, and concerned about her, it made her feel special.

"Well, I think I fainted, but then some strong guy carried me in here and now I'm feeling pretty cozy." Which was a pretty major understatement, given the way her body tingled at the heat emanating from the two men so close to her.

Travis chuckled and rolled toward her, sliding his solid arm around her waist, sending goose bumps quivering along her skin. "I think all three of us are feeling pretty cozy."

Connor rolled toward her. "I know I am." His lips played along the base of her neck. Tingles rushed through her.

"I guess I'm odd man out," Erik said.

Connor's lips moved to her shoulder, sending tingles along her spine.

Travis glided his hand to her breast, and as he caressed it, her nipple peaked against his palm. Erik watched them intently, his cock surging to fullness. Even though Travis and Connor were making her quiver with excitement, she longed to have Erik inside her again.

Connor's gaze locked on Erik's growing cock. "I could take care of that for you."

Erik hesitated, but then settled back on the armchair facing the foot of the bed and wrapped his hand around his cock and stroked.

"That's okay. I can watch for now."

"Well, let's give you something good to watch." Travis pulled the covers off Lindsay, revealing her naked body.

Erik's blue eyes darkened at the sight of her full breasts, the nipples peaking, tight and hard.

Travis glided down the bed, then rolled onto his knees and gazed at Lindsay. She was so beautiful he could hardly wait to make sweet love to her. He cupped her soft breasts in his hands and squeezed them gently, loving the feel of her hard nipples peaking into his palms.

He stroked down her stomach to her intimate folds. His cock twitched when he felt how wet she was. Connor leaned in and lapped at her nipple, then drew it into his mouth. When he sucked, she arched against him. Travis petted her trimmed curls, then his fingertip trailed over her slit, loving the feel of her slick flesh. Connor sucked again and she moaned.

Travis leaned forward and drew her folds apart, then tasted her. Sweet velvet. His tongue darted into her. Her fingers tangled in his long hair as he lapped at her wet flesh. He drew back and smiled at her as he wrapped his hand around Connor's cock and stroked. She watched with an expression of awe. He took the big cock-head into his mouth, watching her. Connor groaned, then licked her nipple.

She watched intently as more of Connor's shaft disappeared into Travis' mouth. As Connor moaned, her nipple slipped from his mouth. Travis stroked her inner thighs as he sucked on Connor. She arched her body, her breast brushing Connor's lips again. Connor licked her, but then rolled back on the bed, caught up in Travis' attention. Travis shifted back to Lindsay, his hand still wrapped around Connor's shaft. With his free hand, he parted her folds and found her clit. He nudged it with his tongue and she moaned, stroking his shoulder-length hair back from his face.

"God, you three are so hot," Erik said.

Travis glanced in the direction of Erik's hoarse voice and saw him stroking his enormous cock as he watched them from the armchair. Lindsay licked her lips, probably longing to feel his big erection in her mouth, just as Travis did. To suck on that bulbous cock-head of his.

Travis moved back to Connor again, this time taking him deep inside, eliciting a groan. Lindsay stroked her hand over Connor's hard, flat stomach and rested her hand against the base of his cock. Travis' lips brushed her fingers every time he glided downward.

He moved back and forth between them, lapping at her clit, then sucking Connor's big cock. When his mouth wasn't on her, his fingers glided over her wet flesh.

God, what could be better than this? Making love to both Connor and this wonderful woman at the same time. Other than Erik joining them.

He licked her sensitive nub, then glided two of his thick fingers into her. At the same time, he still had a firm grip on Connor's erection, gliding up and down the hard flesh. As he pushed his fingers into her, his tongue teased her clit. He was rewarded with a soft moan.

"If you keep doing that"—she sucked in a soft breath—"I'm going to come."

He released Connor and drew her wet folds wider, giving his mouth better access to her clit.

"Do it, doll," Connor said. "Let us watch you come."

As Travis drove his fingers into her faster, she rocked her pelvis against him. Connor licked her hard nipple and when she arched upward, he covered it with his mouth, eliciting a moan. Travis sucked on her button and she tensed, then arched again. Her head fell back and she released a long, languorous moan. Her face glowed with pleasure.

"Oh, God, I want to fuck you right now." Connor nipped at her ear, then rolled to his knees and grabbed her by the hips. He slid her sideways, away from Travis, then settled his knees between her thighs. He grabbed a condom from the bedside table and rolled it on.

"Hey, man. So do I," Travis complained, but in fact, the thought of watching Connor fuck her made his cock ache. He didn't mind waiting.

"Well, fuck this instead." Connor leaned down, settling his muscular chest against her and raising his butt.

Lindsay watched Travis stroke the tight ass Connor presented to him.

"You got it, buddy." Travis knelt behind Connor and pressed his big dick between Connor's ass cheeks and pushed forward, slowly impaling him.

The thought of Travis' cock pushed deep inside Connor's ass sent tremors of excitement through her. Oh, God, this was so wild.

"Oh, fuck, yeah." Connor grabbed his own cock and pressed it against her pussy, then stroked her slick flesh with the hard, hot tip.

Oh, God, she could hardly wait to feel him inside her. He glided into her slowly, stretching her with his enormous cock, until finally he was all the way in. Then he kissed her.

"Now I'm going to fuck you while Travis fucks me," Connor said. "Ready?"

She nodded and Connor drew back, his cock-head stroking her insides, making her quiver. As he drove forward again, she sent Erik a quick glance. His dark gaze was locked on them as he stroked his cock.

She squeezed the big, solid cock inside her. As Connor's cock filled her, she gasped at the pleasure rippling through her. But, oh, God, she couldn't help wondering what it would be like if Erik's cock filled her mouth while the other two fucked her.

Connor glided forward again and she quivered.

"Wait," Erik said.

Connor stopped moving inside her as they both glanced at him.

"Hey, we're kind of busy here," Connor said.

"I know, just one second." He stood up and strode to the side of the bed, then sat down beside her. "Here, sweetheart." He pointed his cock toward her.

Shivers washed through her. God, could the man read her mind?

She tipped her head sideways and licked his tip. He eased closer and guided his cock into her mouth.

It was so wildly sexy. Connor's cock pushing into her. Travis' cock fully impaled in Connor's ass. And now Erik's big shaft stretching her mouth. She sucked on him and he drew back slowly, then glided into her again.

"Fuck, yeah, that is so sexy." Connor moved forward, slowly, his gaze locked on Erik's cock in her mouth, Travis glued to his back.

Lindsay almost came as Connor's cock pushed deep into her again, stretching her passage. It was so insanely erotic. And she couldn't stop thinking about Travis' cock pushed up tight inside Connor.

Connor's cock slid back again, the ridge of his cockhead stroking her vagina. Erik's cock dropped from her mouth as she moaned. She grasped his shaft with her hand and stroked it as Connor continued to thrust into her.

"Oh, God."

Erik stroked her breasts as Connor fucked her. A wave of pleasure rose within her. Erik's cock pulsed in her hand.

"I'm . . ." She gasped as her whole body shuddered. "I'm coming. Ahhh."

Connor thrust into her, Travis moving with him. She continued stroking Erik's cock and it swelled. Her pleasure rose and she began to wail. Her whole consciousness seemed to expand in a flurry of blissful explosions.

"Ah, fuck," Connor groaned, then his face contorted in pleasure.

"Oh, yeah," Travis groaned, following Connor to climax.

As ecstasy rippled through her, she felt Erik's cock twitching wildly in her hand.

Connor and Travis moved away and Erik rolled over her, then filled her with his big cock. He thrust into her, his cock stretching her. Filling her. She gasped, pleasure rising again.

"Oh, God, yes." Joy exploded within her. Again.

Erik groaned, burying his face in her long hair, then he shuddered.

Finally, she collapsed, spent. Erik rested against her.

Then she began to giggle.

Erik rolled sideways, drawing her with him.

"Oh, my God, that was insane," she said.

"But in a good way, right?" Travis asked.

She grinned broadly. "Oh, yes. In a *very* good way."

Lindsay dove into the pool and swam several laps. When she stopped at the deep end of the pool and wiped the water from her eyes, Connor was only a few feet away, treading water. A movement on the diving board caught her attention and she glanced up to see Erik walk the length of the board, bounce, then do a perfect jackknife into the pool.

Wow, he had a body fit for sin. Tall, muscular, and streamlined. He broke the surface and shook his head, scattering droplets of water in all directions. Then his gaze turned to her. Those dark blue eyes stole her breath away every time they locked on her.

Someone moved behind her and she glanced around to see Travis.

His arm brushed hers as he hooked his hand on the side of the pool. "It's a gorgeous day."

The sun shone down hotly, glittering on the clear water of the pool as it rippled and swayed with their movements.

"Would you like to go somewhere," Travis asked, "or just hang out by the pool?"

The thought of leaving this place, where she seemed wrapped in a cocoon of wonderfully decadent sexual freedom, did not appeal to her. Here she could just ignore the rest of the world and get down and dirty with these three sexy men.

"Hang out by the pool. Definitely." She grinned and gazed down at his body in the clear water. "Until something better comes up."

At that, she swam to the shallow end of the pool, then walked up the curved steps and stretched out on the lounge chair. The sun felt good on her naked body, but she'd have to be careful that she didn't get a burn. She'd never sunbathed naked before and didn't really want to experience sunburn on her more intimate parts.

Travis followed her out of the water and settled on the chair beside hers, but sitting up rather than lying down like her. Erik swam lengths and Connor dove into the water one more time.

"May I ask you something, Travis?"

He shrugged. "What do you want to know?"

"I don't mean to pry, but I'm curious about this helpful friend you have. The one who is investing in your company and letting you all live here."

Travis' expression grew guarded.

"Feel free to tell me it's none of my business. It's just that I figured it was Erik, and I was wondering why he's hiding it."

Travis' lips compressed, then he sighed. "No, it's okay. Erik doesn't like to talk about it, and Connor and I respect that, but it should be okay telling you. He comes from a wealthy family, but he was never comfortable with the lifestyle. He always wanted to do something he felt was useful. Give back to the community. So he joined the force and has always lived a very modest life. Then his father died and this penthouse was part of the inheritance. Even though he and his father never saw eye-to-eye, I think he couldn't bear to part with this place." Travis grinned. "Though I think he loves the fact that his father would never approve of the new décor, and for sure he wouldn't approve of what we do here."

She smiled. "Like sharing women."

"Or sharing each other."

Lindsay turned to see Erik and Connor walking up from the pool. Connor grabbed a chair from the patio table and dragged it to sit facing her, while Erik sat a few feet away and dipped his toes in the water.

"Now it's my turn to ask a question." Travis gazed at her. "You said you thought you were going to a girls' weekend away."

"Yes, that's right."

"Then why would you leave your bathing suit behind?" Travis grinned. "I mean, I can't help wondering if you were expecting to go swimming *au natural* with your friends." His grin widened. "And what that might lead to."

"The flaw in your theory is that I didn't think there'd be a private pool."

Connor leaned forward, a glint in his hazel eyes. "That doesn't mean you couldn't sneak out to the pool or hot tub late at night where you could . . . you know"— he winked—"frolic with your friends."

"Naked women frolicking together." Erik smiled broadly. "Now there's something dreams are made of."

Images danced through Lindsay's head of nude women, bodies glistening with water, touching each other, stroking each other's naked skin. In the fantasy, someone's soft hand brushed her breast, then squeezed. Her eyes widened and she shook her head. *My God, what was that?* She'd never *ever* thought of being with women before.

Had being with these sexy men in this uninhibited environment opened up hidden fantasies she didn't even know she had?

Erik winked at her. "Maybe we should call your friend Jill and invite her over, too."

Uncertainty spiked through her, that she wasn't enough for him. Just like she hadn't been enough for Glen. But that was silly. It was just a joke.

She smiled. "If you guys think I'm going to share the wealth, you're crazy."

Connor and Travis both laughed.

Erik grinned broadly. "I'm glad we're keeping you amused."

She smiled. "Well, you are an amusing bunch."

"Speaking of amusement," Erik said. "Since we're all here to live out your sexual fantasy, why don't you tell us what other fantasies you have?"

"Oh, well, I guess that could be . . . fun." Except that she felt awkward sitting here, with three naked men staring at her, talking about what turned her on.

"You don't sound very enthusiastic," Connor said.

"Well, Erik just asked her to reveal her intimate, sexual fantasies." Travis sipped his beer. "She's probably not comfortable doing that."

Erik smiled warmly at her. "Okay, I get that, but why don't you think about it, and if something comes to mind, let us know?"

Think about it. Even an hour later, that's all Lindsay had been able to think about. Especially after these three big naked men had all taken turns applying suntan lotion to her body so she wouldn't burn, then left her wanting more, even though they were also obviously turned on.

Now Travis sat reading a big hardcover book, something about developing apps and cloud computing, while Connor and Erik played cards at the patio table. She watched Connor toss his hand down and grin, then slide the pile of candies and condoms, which they'd been using as poker chips, toward him.

They had a big bowl of individually wrapped hard candies on the table right beside a decorative basket holding brightly colored condom packages, the latter very practical given the purpose of this weekend.

Yellow and green candies were worth one dollar, orange and red worth five, purple worth ten, and a condom packet of any color worth fifty.

What if all of them were playing poker and she ran out of money? What if she really needed the money and was willing to do whatever it took to get it? What if the men knew that, and used the information to their advantage? They might suggest she bet sexual favors to stay in the game. If she lost a hand, she might have to do things to one of the men. Or let one of the men—*or all of them*—do things to her.

Her heart rate increased as she imagined Connor sliding his winnings toward him, a gleam in his eye as he watched her, then gestured for her to come to him.

Having just lost her bet, she stands up and walks toward him, slowly. Reluctantly. Once she stands in front of him, with a big grin on his face, he begins to unfasten the buttons on her blouse. One by one. Revealing her breasts a little at a time. He's never seen her breasts, and of course, she'd never made love with a stranger before, so she quivers as his gaze lingers on the swell of her breasts. Her cheeks burn as he peels open her blouse and stares at her lace-clad breasts, the shameless nipples clearly pushing against the lace.

One of the other men steps behind her and draws her blouse from her shoulders. As she shrugs it away, she notices Erik stepping toward her, unzipping his pants. A shiver dances along her spine.

"You want another drink, Lindsay?"

Lindsay almost jumped at Travis' voice, bringing her back to the here and now. She pushed her sunglasses on top of her head to gaze at him as he stood beside her chair, his own empty beer bottle in his hand.

"Um . . . yes, please."

He took her glass and carried it into the house. She glanced toward the table and saw that Erik was watching her. Something about the way he smiled made her feel he knew exactly what she'd been fantasizing about.

Nine

Erik's cock ached. How could it not with Lindsay watching them play cards with that look of hunger in her eyes? He would love to invite her to play poker with them. To role-play that she was broke and had to win at all costs, and where that would lead. She'd been thinking about fantasies since he'd suggested it, but this was the strongest. It was clearly a fantasy she could get into. And his throbbing cock testified to how much it turned him on.

"Erik, your turn to deal."

Connor's voice dragged Erik's attention back to the table, and the deck of cards lying in front of him.

"Hey, Lindsay, would you like to join us?" Erik asked.

She glanced at him. "Uh, sure." She walked to the table and settled into the chair across from him.

"But, I was thinking we could take it a step further?" he said. "I think there's a lot of potential here for some role-playing."

Lindsay's eyes widened a little as she gazed at him. "What do you have in mind?"

"Well, I was thinking you could be a young woman who's in desperate trouble and needs money to get out of it. You join a card game with some wealthy men—that's us—hoping to win the money you need. And, of course, when you start losing, maybe you bet things a *lady* shouldn't bet."

Erik could tell she was almost salivating at the thought.

"Well, uh . . ." Her cheeks flushed a soft rose color. "That could be fun."

Erik chuckled. He was quite certain it would be very fun indeed.

Erik stepped out of the elevator to the penthouse. He'd driven Lindsay to her apartment because she wanted to pick up something to wear for the fantasy scenario. On the way up the elevator, Erik had made a couple of calls to set things up for the evening and texted Lindsay where to meet them.

He walked past the kitchen and down the hall toward his room to change.

"You seem to be enjoying Lindsay's company."

At Connor's voice, Erik paused outside the open door to Travis' room.

"Isn't that the point of this weekend?" Travis asked.

"Sure, but I've never seen you allow a woman so close. That hug out on the deck . . . that was clearly intense. And the way you two were talking so intently by the pool . . ."

Erik knew he shouldn't be eavesdropping, but Connor's concerned tone kept him frozen to the spot.

"Is that a problem?" Travis asked.

Alarm bells clamored in Erik's head. Would having Lindsay here cause issues between them?

"No, I don't mean that, I'm just . . ."

"Connor, you don't need to be jealous," Travis said. "Whatever happens between Lindsay and me won't affect how I feel about you. I promise."

Those well-intentioned words didn't set Erik's mind at ease. When people got intimate, unpredictable stuff happened.

His stomach clenched as he remembered the pain Becci had brought to them. When she had decided Erik wasn't the man of her dreams, instead of just walking away, she'd tried to convince Connor and Travis to ditch Erik. She'd loved being the center of attention of three men and wasn't about to give it up just because she didn't want Erik anymore. She'd decided she could settle for two men and so she had started a campaign to tear their relationship apart. Her selfishness had caused anxiety and pain for all three of them. Erik didn't think Lindsay would ever do something so selfish, but that didn't mean her presence couldn't cause major problems.

"Okay, good," Connor said. "We've never actually talked about where our relationship is going, but I guess I always assumed we'd stay together. I like what we have and I don't want to lose you."

"And what about Erik?"

"Come on. We both know that Erik will probably wind up married with kids. If that relationship includes us, that's great, but who knows?"

Erik's gut clenched as shock quivered through him. He knew Connor and Travis had had a relationship long before they met him, but he hadn't realized they considered him a dispensable part of the trio.

Lindsay sat at the bar in the casino, feeling a little out of place, especially dressed in her boxy gray business suit and white blouse, with her hair pinned up. Glasses were the finishing touch to the dowdy librarian look. Around her, colored lights flashed and people milled around the gambling tables.

The bartender placed a tall drink in front of her. "From that gentleman." He took away her empty glass.

Lindsay glanced at Travis who sat down on the stool next to her, a short, wide glass in his hand. This was the start of their role-playing. She was supposed to wait until one of the guys showed up, then tell him her unhappy story.

Wow, Travis looked exceptionally gorgeous in his tailored suit, which set off his broad shoulders. Usually, his long, dark hair softened his square jawline, but he'd tied it back, so his face looked even more masculine—and devastatingly handsome—than usual.

"You look troubled," Travis said.

She glanced at the drink and took a sip. "I don't usually talk to strangers about my problems."

"Yes, but I'm so charming, how can you resist?" His broad, white smile and the glitter in his eyes did make him difficult to resist.

He leaned in close. "Look, I know we're supposed to act out the part where you tell me your partner ran off with all the money from your bookstore and now you're broke, then I'll invite you to a big-deal poker game where we'll offer you credit and you can win back your money. If you want to go through all that, I will, but instead, we could just enjoy each other's company for a few minutes."

She smiled. "Sure. I don't need to act it out. As long as we play the part when we head to the poker game."

"Sure thing."

He slid his arm around her and drew her against his body. "Right now, I just want to be close to you for a few minutes, where I don't have to share you with anyone."

The warmth of his hard, masculine body so close to hers sent her hormones dancing. She'd started off this weekend on a date with Erik, and she'd hoped that their relationship could continue, but being with his two friends definitely complicated things. Especially with Travis, since they seemed to have connected on some deeper level.

"But I thought sharing was what this weekend was all about," she murmured as he nuzzled her neck. Tingles danced along her spine as his lips brushed her skin lightly.

"It's also about the sex," he murmured in her ear, "but we don't have to be doing it the whole time."

He cupped her cheek, and tilted her face up, then brushed his lips over hers. His tongue glided along her lips, then pressed inside. She returned his kiss, her tongue swirling against his. Her heart rate increased and she longed for him to pull her into a tighter embrace. To feel his body the length of hers.

He released her with a smile. "It's time to go to our *private* game."

She gazed at him in a daze, wondering if he'd gotten a room for the two of them or something, then realized he meant the poker game. With Erik and Connor.

"Okay." She took a sip of her drink, then he offered his elbow and she hooked her arm around it.

Lindsay followed Travis across the loud, crowded room to the elevator. When the doors opened, several people followed them inside. Travis pressed the number for the floor above the casino.

The doors opened and she followed Travis off the elevator.

"Where are we going?" she asked.

He gestured in front of them. She walked down a

short hall to an atrium with several meeting rooms. Travis knocked on the second door on the left.

"Come in."

Connor opened the door. "There you are."

Inside, Erik sat at a big oval table made of rich, dark, gleaming wood, and the chairs were leather. There was a sitting area with a couch and easy chairs at the other end of the room. A bar fridge stood off to the side.

"So who have we here?" Erik asked.

"I thought we needed a fourth for our game."

Connor and Erik looked devastatingly handsome in their classy dark suits, ties, and white shirts. And imposing.

Even though she stood before them in an unflattering, boxy suit, with glasses on and her hair tied back like a cliché librarian, the glitter in their eyes, especially Connor's, sent heat shimmering through her.

"Of course. And what a lovely addition." Erik held out his hand for a handshake. As soon as his big hand enveloped hers, she felt shivers dance along her skin.

There was something about this role-playing—pretending they didn't know each other—that made everything more exciting.

"I'm . . . uh . . . Lindsay Reed."

"And I'm Connor." Connor shook her hand next. Before he released it, his finger brushed against the underside of her wrist, sending quivers through her.

"A glass of wine?" Connor asked.

"Yes, please."

Travis drew back one of the rolling leather chairs and gestured for her to sit down. She set her purse on the table and dug inside for the chips they'd given her before she left the penthouse. The ones she was pretending to have left over from gambling at the blackjack table. She set them on the table, but her stack was extremely tiny compared to the huge stacks Erik, Travis, and Connor had.

The faster for me to lose and get to the exciting bit. Excitement quivered through her.

Connor set a stemmed glass of white wine in front of her and handed a tall glass of beer to Travis. Erik shuffled the cards and dealt them out.

Lindsay won the first hand with a pair of kings, but lost the second hand even though she had three twos. Travis, with his four sixes, scooped away the pile of chips including half her winnings. Over the next several hands she lost more than she won, until finally she only had fifty dollars left.

Connor dealt the cards and she picked up her hand. Just a mishmash, but when she drew new cards, she wound up with all spades. Everyone started betting and the pot grew. Unfortunately, Erik raised an amount she couldn't cover.

"It looks like Lindsay could be out of the game," Connor said.

"That's true." Travis smiled. "If you lose this hand, you've got nothing left."

Erik raised an eyebrow. "So, Miss Reed, how much do you want to stay in the game?"

"I'd like to keep playing until I win the money I need."

Erik sat back in his chair and smiled. "I have an idea. Why don't we give you back all the money you have in the pot, and you can bet something else?"

"Like what?" she asked innocently.

Connor eyed her. "That's a very nice suit, but I would love to see you lose it, and take off the blouse."

A tremor of excitement rippled through her at the thought of sitting here with the men in their full suits and her in her bra and skirt.

She stared at the pot, as if carefully considering the situation. "Okay, let's do it."

Travis grabbed her chips from the pot and slid them back to her. She stacked them in front of her.

"So, Lindsay, what do you have?"

She grinned. "I'm sorry to tell you boys that . . ." She flipped over her cards. "I have a flush."

"That is too bad." Connor didn't look disappointed at all as he turned over his cards. "But as it turns out, my full house beats your flush."

He dropped his cards faceup on the table. A pair of eights and three jacks.

Travis and Erik both laughed as they tossed their cards aside.

She drew in a breath and stood up, then removed her suit jacket. Her fingers found the top button of her blouse and she released it. Their gazes locked on her hands. She found the next button and released that one. Their gazes dropped lower. She continued to unbutton her blouse until it hung open, revealing a couple of inches of skin.

As she slipped off her blouse, goose bumps danced across her flesh. Now she sat in her straight skirt and low-cut, pink lace bra. With her glasses and her hair still pulled tight behind her head, she felt half librarian and half virginal temptress. Connor handed her the deck and she dealt out the cards. She lost the hand and realized they hadn't stated what she'd lose this time.

She stood up. "I assume you'd like me to lose the skirt."

"Actually, no." Erik smiled. "Instead, I'd rather you take off your panties."

"Oh, yeah." Connor grinned widely.

With the length of her skirt, they wouldn't see a thing. But when she stood up to slip off her panties, she realized it wouldn't be as simple as she'd thought. She had to hike the skirt up pretty high before she could get ahold of them and pull them down, and every male eye scrutinized the skin she bared. Finally, she dropped them to the floor, then she opened her purse to slip them inside.

"Hey, I think the winner should get to keep those." Connor held out his hand.

She placed her crumpled panties in his big palm.

Connor closed his fingers around them. "Mmm. They're still warm." He held them to his cheek, his eyes gleaming. "And you're naked under that skirt."

From the way all of them were looking at her, she realized that just the thought of her not wearing panties had them all turned on. If she gazed under the table right now, she would surely see tent poles in every pair of trousers.

She shifted a little in her seat, the wool of her skirt brushing against her folds. In fact, it was turning her on, too.

She won the next two hands, probably because the men were very distracted, their gazes alternating from lingering on her breasts and drifting to the table, as if they thought if they concentrated hard enough, they'd be able to see through the table and the wool of her skirt.

Travis won the next hand and smiled. "I think Lindsay might be getting a little cold with no panties, so I'd like her to put some on."

Her eyebrows arched. "You want me to put my panties back on?"

"Not *your* panties." He stood up and grabbed a briefcase from under the table. He opened it and took out a small box, then handed it to her.

She peered inside to find black satin-and-lace panties.

"Very pretty." She lifted them from the box and stood up.

"Wait, don't forget this." Travis reached for the panties, then slid a little black device into a pocket in the front. "Now put them on."

She took the panties from him, eyeing what she realized was probably a bullet vibrator, then pulled them on. The vibrator sat nestled against her.

Travis held up a black device small enough to fit in

the palm of his hand. "Now whoever wins a hand can hold the remote control."

"Remote control to . . ." The vibrator began to move against her clit. She dropped into the chair, her eyes wide at the intense sensation flooding through her.

Erik chucked. "I think you'd better turn it off before she loses it."

"I'd like to watch her lose it." Connor's smile widened as he watched her.

Ten

Lindsay had to concentrate just to stop herself from slumping in the chair and letting herself go to the pleasure. But the vibrations stopped. She pushed herself straighter, then took a deep sip of her wine.

"You expect me to play cards with this thing on?"

"We're distracted. Why shouldn't you be?" Travis winked.

While they played the next hand, the vibrator periodically leapt to life, quivered against her clit for a few seconds, then stopped. Connor won the next hand and ramped it up, giving her long bouts of quivering pleasure. She could barely think straight let alone concentrate on which cards to play. When Travis won, he kept her on the edge of her seat because he didn't turn it on at all. She kept waiting for it. And *wanting* it.

On Erik's win, he turned it up to vibrate steadily against her clit, sending her pleasure higher and higher.

She slumped in the chair, aware of the male gazes watching her hungrily, but just barely. Pleasure swamped her senses, rising and rising. When she was just a breath away from an orgasm, the vibrator stopped.

"Nooo."

Erik's smile stretched across his face. He stood up and rounded the table, then took her hand and drew her to her feet. Her knees were rubbery, but she stood. He reached behind her and unhooked her bra, then drew it from her body. Her nipples puckered in the cool air, then ached at the heat of his gaze.

He stroked over one nipple and she arched against his fingers.

"Fuck, I can't stand it." Connor stood up and walked toward her as he unzipped his pants and pulled out his big, hard cock. "I want to fuck her so bad." He unfastened her skirt and tugged it downward. It dropped to the floor, revealing her pink garter belt and stockings.

Erik cupped her breasts, and squeezed gently, then turned her toward the table. He tugged her panties off, then stroked her bare behind. She quivered inside, standing there basically naked in the middle of these three fully suited men.

Connor dropped an empty condom packet on the table, then a moment later placed his hand on her back and pressed her forward, until she leaned over the table. She rested her hands against the hard surface, then gasped as she felt his hot, hard flesh glide against her.

"She is so fucking wet." At that, Connor drove into her.

His big cock stretched her as it went in deep.

"Oh, yes." She quivered.

He drew back and drove forward again. His hands found her breasts and he cupped them, teasing the nipples, then pulled her tight to his body and nuzzled her temple. "You are so fucking hot I'm going to come any second."

He drew back and plunged into her again. And again. He groaned, then shuddered against her. She squeezed his cock inside her. Her own orgasm swept through her and she moaned.

Connor pulled out and Travis stepped behind her. His cock drove into her and he thrust over and over again. Another orgasm catapulted through her and he groaned in release.

When he pulled free, she expected Erik to take his place, but instead, he took her hand and led her to the couch at the side of the room. He sat down and unzipped his pants. His huge erection stood like a rocket ready to launch. As soon as he rolled a condom on, she knelt over his lap. He leaned forward and captured one of her hard nipples in his mouth and suckled. She cradled his head against her, moaning at the exquisite pleasure of his mouth around her and the delicate pull of his sucking.

"Oh, God, I'm going to come again."

At her words, he pressed his cock to her wet folds and pulled her down on him. He wrapped his hands around her waist and guided her body up and down. His cock-head stroked her insides, thrilling her. She squeezed as he thrust into her. Bliss pummeled through her, building. Spreading.

"Oh, God, I'm going to . . ." Pleasure erupted inside her and she wailed. She rode the wave of pleasure, then slumped on Erik's chest.

But he was still hard inside her. She pushed herself up and started to ride him again.

He chuckled. "It's okay, sweetheart. I'm good."

"Actually, I can be of help." Connor helped her to slide onto the couch beside Erik, then he leaned against the arm of the couch.

Erik stood up and pressed his cock to Connor's anus and slowly eased inside. Travis dropped down on the couch in front of Connor and licked his cock, then took it in his mouth.

She sat in fascination, her gaze locked on Connor's cock gliding into Travis' mouth. Behind Connor, Erik thrust deep, impaling him. Erik's cock drove in and out of Connor until both men groaned their release. Travis swallowed as Connor came in his mouth.

She was so turned on again, she grabbed Travis' hard cock and tugged him toward her. She lay back on the couch and he straddled her, then drove his cock deep inside. She squeezed him inside.

"God, yes. That's so good."

He pumped into her, filling her deeply.

Pleasure swelled through her, carrying her higher. "I can't believe you can actually . . ."

Travis drew back and thrust again.

". . . you can make me . . . oh . . ."

Travis' cock swelled inside her, stretching her vagina.

". . . come . . . again . . ." Joy pulsed through her. She gasped, then wailed.

They collapsed together on the couch.

Lindsay started giggling, totally giddy from the practically nonstop orgasms. And the fact she was lying here, totally naked, while the three men were fully dressed.

"You guys are totally insane," she babbled between breaths.

Travis drew away, smiling. "And you love it."

She grinned, not even bothering to deny it. He pulled her to her feet and into his arms. He removed her glasses as she gazed into his heated brown eyes. He cupped her face and drew her forward, then captured her lips. His kiss was gentle and hungry at the same time. His tongue glided into her mouth and consumed her.

"You know, you spent last night alone with Erik. How about you give me a chance tonight?"

Some of her hair had escaped the clip at the back of her head and he stroked loose tendrils behind her ear. At the tenderness of his touch, she was a heartbeat from saying yes.

"Hey, buddy, don't you think the winner should wind up with the prize?" Erik said.

She could see the disappointment in Travis' eyes as Erik drew her into his arms, but when he kissed her possessively, all thought melted away.

Lindsay gazed at the wonderful view of the city from the window of the restaurant atop the ritzy hotel. The sun was just beginning to set so they'd have a lovely backdrop for their dinner conversation. A tuxedo-clad host led them to a curved booth in a cozy, intimate corner.

As she slid along the leather upholstered bench, she was glad she'd brought her sundress to change into before they'd left the conference room. Negotiating the curve of the bench would have been awkward in the tight skirt. And thank heavens she'd had extra panties in her bag, since Connor had insisted on keeping the ones he'd won during the poker game.

A waiter came by promptly and lit the candle in the mosaic holder at the center of the table. The light glowed warmly through the amber-tinted iridescent glass.

"Red wine?" the waiter asked, holding an open bottle.

"Yes, please." She watched him fill the tall, delicate stemmed glass at her place setting.

He filled each of the other glasses, too.

"I called ahead and ordered filet mignon for all of us," Travis said. "Is that okay with you, Lindsay?"

"That sounds lovely."

The waiter nodded. "Very good. I'll bring the first course."

"Nice place." She unfolded the cloth napkin from her plate and laid it across her lap. This restaurant looked very expensive. With the penthouse they lived in, this expensive restaurant, and the fact they'd rented a meeting room at the casino for their role-playing, she knew Erik must be extremely well-off. She felt a surge of warmth when she thought of him going to work as a cop every day simply because he wanted to help people.

"It has a nice ambience," Travis agreed.

The waiter appeared and placed a platter down with baguette slices covered with a blend of tomato chunks and herbs topped with small chunks of white cheese. "This is a bruschetta made with herbed goat cheese, fresh plum tomatoes, olive oil, and balsamic vinegar," he said, placing small plates in front of each of them. "Enjoy."

He topped off their wineglasses, then disappeared again. Lindsay picked up a slice from the platter, then took a nibble. The tangy flavor filled her mouth.

"Mmm. This is good." She finished the slice, then sipped her wine before helping herself to another.

She took another bite and swallowed. "Have you done this before?" She glanced at Travis. "I mean, invited a woman for a weekend like this?"

"Would you be offended if we said we have?" Connor sipped his wine, then picked up a third slice of bruschetta.

"Offended? Of course not." But she did feel disappointed, despite herself.

"Liar." Erik stared at her with a grin.

"Well, it would have felt more special if I'd been the

only one, but . . ." She shrugged. "That's just my ego talking."

"Lindsay, you are special," Erik said.

"Sure, I know. All of the women you've been with are special."

"Lindsay."

She lifted her gaze from her wineglass to Erik's intent blue eyes.

"You are special."

She shifted in her seat. She didn't know how to behave under his intense stare. Didn't know what to say.

The waiter arrived and took away the empty platter, then replaced it with another. "Maryland crab cakes served with a green onion sauce." He cleared away their small plates and set out clean ones, then disappeared with quiet efficiency.

She didn't say anything as she enjoyed the crispy crab cakes with the zesty sauce.

"Lindsay, I didn't mean to make you uncomfortable." Erik watched her as he sipped his wine.

"No. I'm not." She was lying, but what else could she do? She smiled. "Well, *I've* never done this before and I assure you all, you're very special."

Connor laughed.

"So why did you decide to become a police officer?" she asked Erik.

"I guess I wanted to do something worthwhile."

She smiled. "That's a good reason. Your family must be very proud of you.

Connor choked on his crab cake and Erik sent him a sharp glance.

"No. My father was very different than me. His idea of a good living was making as much money as possible. He frowned on my decision to serve the public. He preferred to have people serve him."

She frowned. "Are you saying your father disapproved of you becoming a police officer?"

Erik laughed without humor. "That's an understatement."

Erik clearly had issues with his family. Perhaps that was why he was so guarded. He was protective of his emotions, and very careful who he let in.

She couldn't conceive of a father who wouldn't be beaming-proud of a son who decided to become a police officer. Concerned, perhaps, about his safety. But not disapproving. She gazed at Erik's strong face, noting the tight set of his square jaw. She hadn't missed the wounded look in his deep blue eyes, either, when he'd talked about his father. Since Erik had inherited the penthouse and they'd only moved in a few weeks ago, she assumed his father had died recently. She wished she could get him to open up about it.

"Travis told me your father passed away. How long ago was it?" she asked solemnly.

"A few months ago," Erik said.

"I'm so sorry, Erik."

Erik simply nodded.

Silence hung over them for a long moment.

The raw pain in Erik's eyes tore at her heart. He was clearly still trying to come to terms with his father's death, both emotionally and how having his father's legacy—his money—would affect his life.

"Well, this is a downer." Connor took a swallow of his wine. "How about we talk about something fun?"

"Like what?" Travis asked.

"I was thinking"—he raised his eyebrows and grinned—"maybe we can talk about what we'll do when we get home."

Lindsay laughed. Connor could be outrageous at times. Of course, that was part of his charm.

She nibbled at her crab cake. "Why don't we wait until we get home to figure that out? Spontaneity can be fun."

"You like spontaneity?" Connor grinned and tugged the tablecloth up. "I'll show you spontaneity." He slid downward, disappearing under the table.

Eleven

Lindsay glanced around quickly to see if anyone had noticed, but no one seemed to be looking their way. It helped that they were in a nice quiet corner.

Just as she felt him stroke his hand over her knee, the waiter arrived with the wine bottle. As Connor stroked up her thigh, the waiter topped up her glass, then the others.

"The main course is nearly ready." The waiter took away her empty plate. "Should I wait until the other gentleman returns before I bring it?"

She had to fight the effect of the quivering sensations rippling through her as Connor pressed her knees apart and glided his hand farther up her leg, desperately trying to keep her expression flat. The waiter cleared the rest of the plates.

"I think he might be a few minutes yet." Erik glanced at her, then grinned. "Maybe hold off for about ten minutes."

She felt Connor's fingertip stroke along the crotch of her panties and she almost jumped.

"Very good, sir." The waiter walked away, carrying the dirty plates in one hand and the wine bottle in the other.

Connor's finger slipped under her panties and he stroked her already slick flesh. She drew in a breath.

Travis leaned forward. "So, Lindsay, are you enjoying your appetizer?"

Connor's finger slipped inside her and her breathing grew ragged.

"I believe she is." Erik smiled, watching her face intently.

She felt Connor's slightly raspy cheek brush her upper thigh, then he pulled aside the fabric and his mouth covered her. She couldn't stop a sigh from escaping her lips.

"Oh, yeah. She's enjoying it," Travis agreed.

Connor's tongue teased her clit, then he dipped another finger inside. A swirl of fog spun around her as he glided his fingers in and out, all the while licking her clit. She grasped Travis' hand, which lay on the seat beside her and clung to it as Connor pulsed into her. Pleasure swamped her senses. Connor's tongue flicked rapidly and his fingers moved faster.

"Oh, God," she whispered. She squeezed Travis' hand in a vise grip. Despite the tight hold she kept on the rising pleasure, an orgasm blossomed through her. Quiet and sublime. She slumped back against the bench seat and sucked in air, trying to watch her surroundings through half-lidded eyes while riding the wave of exquisite sensations.

Finally, slowly, her sense of time and composure returned. Connor's mouth lifted from her and he positioned the crotch of her panties back in place. Erik picked up a cloth napkin and discreetly slid his hand under the table. Connor slid back into his seat, wiping his mouth with the napkin, then set it down on his lap with a big grin on his face.

"Spontaneous enough for you?" he asked.

She nodded, uncertain she could speak without a quiver in her voice. She pushed herself upright and grabbed her water, then took a sip.

The waiter returned seconds later.

Oh, God, please don't let him have noticed Connor gliding up from under the table.

But the waiter made no indication of noticing anything out of the ordinary.

"Are you ready for your entrée?" he asked.

"Yes, please. That last course stimulated my appetite." Connor grinned.

"Of course, sir."

The waiter left again and Lindsay slumped back against the seat. "Connor, you're terrible."

"Really? You can't tell me you didn't like that."

"That's true." Erik sipped his wine and winked at her. "Both Travis and I saw clear evidence that you enjoyed it."

"If you really didn't enjoy it, then"—Connor lifted the tablecloth again—"I should give it another try."

She giggled, still a little giddy from the orgasm. "You really are terrible. In an utterly delightful way."

"I bet he's *wet* your appetite for more." Travis winked at her.

Connor grinned. "Yes, definitely wet." He leaned in close and nuzzled her neck.

She straightened up as she saw the waiter approach. He set a plate in front of her with a thick round steak, some small roast potatoes, and a bundle of asparagus wrapped in bacon. She gazed at the beautifully arranged food and waited in anticipation while the waiter placed plates in front of her companions.

The men were certainly treating her like someone special.

Erik stared at the orange and mauve sky as the sun sank below the horizon. He was still unsettled by the conversation about his father. He had always wished his father had loved him for who he was rather than trying to mold him into another version of himself.

A hand brushed his sleeve. He turned to see Lindsay gazing at him.

"Are you okay?"

He smiled. "Of course."

Her lovely blue eyes, so full of kindness and concern, almost made him believe that she could be the one who would love him no matter what. Whether he had money or not. Despite having a quirky ability that sent most women running for the hills.

But he knew better. He just wasn't meant to have a long-term relationship with a woman. Even when he was sure it would all work out, it didn't. But that didn't mean he couldn't enjoy being with a woman from time to time. Especially a sexy, delightful woman like Lindsay.

He watched her take a bite of steak from her fork, her soft pink lips wrapping around the metal tines, then the fork slipping from her mouth. Her curved, feminine jawline moved as she chewed, making her lips seem to caress each other. He could imagine gliding his tongue between those lips and slipping into her silky warm mouth.

The memory of her in orgasm while Connor licked her sweet pussy, and the knowledge that she was still wet with arousal made it very difficult to concentrate on his steak. All he wanted to taste right now was her. He was sure Travis was in the same state—probably Connor, too, even though he'd tasted her only moments ago—because they both tucked into their steaks with a diligent concentration to finish quickly.

Erik took his last bite and placed his knife and fork on his plate. Lindsay continued eating, only half done. A moment later, she glanced around and noticed all the men were finished, while she still had half her dinner left. She finished her asparagus, then put down her fork with a smile.

"I think I'll need a doggy bag."

Travis glanced around and the waiter approached the table promptly.

"The check, please."

"Of course, sir."

By the time Erik had signed the credit card slip, his cock was aching at the thought of what was to come. He slid out of the booth, then offered his arm when she stood up. She rested her soft hand on his arm and accompanied him from the restaurant, on the heels of Travis and Connor.

"I'll drive," Connor offered, and Travis handed him the keys.

"I sit in the back with Lindsay." Erik ignored Travis' disappointed expression and opened the back passenger door for Lindsay, then got in the other side.

As soon as he sat beside her and closed the door, he glanced at her long, sexy legs so close to his and remembered Connor sliding under the table, and imagined what Connor had been doing to her. How he must have slid his hand up those silky thighs and spread them apart, then pressed his tongue to her slick flesh. Her sweet pussy was probably still wet.

He longed to glide his hand under her skirt to find out. But a bigger desire pushed through him. He slid his arm around her and drew her close. He needed to feel her lips on his. To feel her in his arms.

She gazed up at him and her silvery-blue eyes shone

with a similar need. He drew her into his arms and her lips met his with enthusiasm. The heat of more than desire swept through him, knocking him off balance. He wanted her. But it was more than sex. More than mere lust.

He *wanted* her. In his bed. In his life.

The tip of her tongue teased his lips and he thrust his tongue into her mouth, needing to feel her around him.

These feelings were so intense . . . so potent. . . . He had never wanted a woman this badly before.

He knew he should pull away. Knew that this was dangerous to his happiness. But he didn't want to. Not now. Tomorrow this would all end. She would leave and then it would just be him, Travis, and Connor again. Until the next time they decided to share a woman.

He drove his tongue deeper, his lips moving on hers with passion, while he enjoyed her murmurs of pleasure and the softness of her in his arms.

Why not enjoy it while she was here? He missed having a relationship with a woman. Having the same woman in his bed regularly. But he'd decided that kind of relationship wasn't for him. Not in the long run. It led to pain and he didn't need that.

His heart clenched at the memory of Cyndi striding to the door, dragging her wheeled suitcase behind her. Before she had closed the door, with tears running from her eyes, she'd turned and told him how sorry she was. But she'd still left. She was the first woman he'd really loved and she'd broken his heart.

Becci was the second, and her departure was even

worse because she'd tried to take Travis and Connor with her. The intense need for Lindsay rushing through him right now was probably just a result of sensing her desires, making his feelings more intense than they actually were. After tomorrow, once Lindsay was gone, he'd be back to normal. But, damn it, he'd enjoy every last scrap of pleasure now, even the intensity of it—especially the intensity of it—augmented by her desires.

Why not enjoy all the benefits of his gift?

Lindsay melted into the phenomenal kiss. Erik's hands moved over her back, glided along her arms, then slid to her back again were drew her tighter to his body. Her nipples ached as her breasts as he crushed against his rock-hard chest.

She'd thought he'd ravish her as soon as the car started moving, but she hadn't expected this. She'd thought his hands would find her breasts and tease her to distraction, or slip under her skirt to explore the slickness left behind by the orgasm Connor had brought her to in the restaurant.

This passionate merging of mouths, his tongue possessing her with deep, masterful strokes, left her absolutely breathless.

The car stopped.

"Hey, you two. We're here," Connor announced.

She gazed at Erik. His midnight-blue eyes gleamed with desire.

He smiled. "Now I have to walk across the lobby

with this." He took her hand and set it on the hard bulge in his pants.

She giggled, still giddy from the tumultuous emotions swirling through her.

She'd never been kissed like that before. She couldn't drag her gaze from his. It had to mean something. Was he falling for her? Was she falling for him?

Her heart swelled. Of course she was. She'd known it ever since she'd seen him in his police uniform. The attraction had been palpable. Even the first time she'd run into him in the elevator, she'd felt it. But even more than physical attraction, she was drawn to the man he was. His strong sense of duty. His sense of humor. And the way he made her feel.

He opened the car door and offered his hand to help her from the car. She stepped out and he kept her hand enveloped in his as they followed Connor and Travis across the parking garage to the elevator.

And it was amazing how he always seemed to know what she was thinking.

She glanced at his profile. Did the way he'd been behaving mean that maybe there was a possible future? Would he give them a chance to explore a relationship that lasted longer than this weekend?

The elevator doors opened and they stepped inside.

Oh, man, she was getting way ahead of herself. She didn't even know if she wanted to get into a relationship right now. After all, Glen had done a number on her self-esteem. Not only had she caught him with two other women, but she was pretty sure that he'd cheated on her several times before. Clearly, she had not been pretty enough or smart enough to keep him interested. And, when she'd caught him with the two women, he'd told her he'd done it because she was *boring* in bed.

She smiled. There was nothing boring about what she'd been doing with Erik and the guys. In fact, being with them had undone some of the damage—not just from Glen, but everything in her life that had made her feel less than special. Audrey constantly criticized her hair, how she dressed, how she behaved.

Even her job. Audrey thought that with a college education, Lindsay should be doing better than "filing papers," as she put it. She didn't realize that Lindsay actually managed a staff to track physical documents across a huge international corporation.

Although the guys might tease her by calling her a librarian, she didn't feel the need to prove herself to them. They seemed happy with her just the way she was.

Lindsay, you are special.

Erik's words swelled through her, straight to her heart. He thought she was special. And around him—and Connor and Travis—she *felt* special. She would like to continue to feel that way.

Lindsay gazed up at Erik. His eyes gleamed with need and he captured her lips again. When the elevator doors opened, he swept her into his arms and carried her into the penthouse and down the hall.

When he entered the master bedroom and closed the door, she could hear Travis' voice.

"You know, it's not fair that you get the woman again tonight."

Twelve

Lindsay felt the soft pillow top of the mattress beneath her back as Erik laid her gently on the bed. Her gaze drifted to the giant bulge forming in his pants.

"You're driving me crazy, woman, looking at me like you could eat me up."

"Mmm. I could do exactly that."

"Okay, hold that thought."

He disappeared into the en suite bathroom and returned a few moments later with several condom packets in his hand. He fanned them out in front of her.

"What flavor would you like?"

She grinned. "Seriously? Flavored condoms?" She glanced at the different colored packets.

From the labels on the plastic, she could see there was strawberry, chocolate, vanilla, grape, banana, cola, and mint. She plucked the grape one from his hand and ripped open the packet. The scent of grape tickled her nose.

He raised an eyebrow. "Not chocolate?"

She grinned as she unzipped his pants and reached inside for the hot, hard shaft. She drew it out and placed the purple condom on the end. "I'm feeling adventurous." She rolled the condom down.

Adventurous was becoming her usual behavior. No doubt about it, staying for this weekend was the best decision she'd made in a long time.

She licked the tip of him and a grapey taste tingled her tongue. "Mmm. I like."

She wrapped her lips around him and drew his cockhead into her mouth, then sucked him like a popsicle.

His hand clamped around her head, his fingers gliding through her hair.

"Oh, God. Me, too."

She sucked him hard, loving the size of him in her mouth and the delightful novelty of a flavored cock. She glided down, taking him deep into her throat, then turned her head back and forth, rotating his cock inside her throat.

"Oh, God, sweetheart. That's . . . ahhh . . ."

She squeezed him inside her mouth.

"Incredible."

She slid the length of him, then dove deep again. Then she bobbed up and down, squeezing and licking him as she moved.

"Mmm, you're so tasty. I don't think I want to stop." She licked downward, past the condom and licked his balls. Gently, she drew one into her mouth, then the other as she stroked his cock with her hand.

"Sweetheart, you are driving me wild."

She grinned. "Good. Because when I'm around you, I feel wild. And very sexy."

His hands grasped her arms and suddenly she found herself on her back with him above her.

"That's because you are wild and sexy." His lips clamped onto hers and he kissed her until she was breathless, his tongue driving deep, then swirling inside her. "And I can't seem to get enough of you."

He stripped of her clothes, then his and prowled over her again. His cock dragged along her stomach, then suddenly it glided inside her, filling her with his awesome length.

"Oh, God, you feel so good inside me." Her cheeks felt flushed and she could barely catch her breath. She wanted him to drive into her, again and again, until she screamed so loud the neighbors would complain. Or call the police.

As he drew back slowly, his cock caressing her passage as it withdrew, she thought about the fact that Erik was a police officer and that thought sent a quiver through her. God, he probably had handcuffs around here somewhere.

He stared down at her, surprise rippling across his features. And a definite gleam in his eye.

God damn, but she was beginning to think the man could read her mind.

Then he drove forward and all her thoughts scattered.

She tightened around him, wanting him deep inside her. He thrust and thrust until she could barely catch her breath. Then the orgasm washed over her in an ecstatic wave.

"Oh, God, yes." She clung to him as she wailed long and loud.

He kept driving into her. Deep and hard. Fast. Filling her. Driving up her pleasure until it exploded into total bliss. His arms tightened around her and he groaned his release.

They lay gasping in each other's arms. He rolled to her side, pulling her tight against him, as if he didn't want to let her go. Which was fine with her because she wasn't going anywhere.

When she smiled and gazed up at him, her breath dissipated at the loving look in his eyes. Her heart swelled with happiness. After Glen, she'd decided there weren't any guys out there worth getting involved with.

Until now.

Erik held Lindsay tight to his chest, loving the feel of this woman against him. Her soft body against his hard one. Loving how they fit together.

But, damn it, he didn't want to be involved with a female. She would only hurt him in the end, just like all the others. He gazed at her glowing face and his heart ached.

Not that she'd mean to. None of them had meant to hurt him, not even Becci. They just couldn't handle what he could do.

But what if he just told her? Right now. Blurted it out.

Lindsay, I can read your sexual fantasies. When something arouses you, I can see it and feel it.

You mean, you can read my thoughts? she'd probably ask, just like most of the women he'd told.

No, it's not like that. I just get images of what you imagine.

Then he'd demonstrate. Get her fantasizing about something and tell her verbatim what she was imagining. That's when they usually freaked out. That's when they feared he was digging around in their minds and they ended it. First Cyndi and then Becci.

But what if Lindsay was different?

As hope swelled in him, he remembered Cyndi. How he'd been so sure she was *the one*. How he'd believed she really loved him.

But he'd been wrong. And the pain had been intense.

With the powerful connection he felt with Lindsay, that pain would be even worse. If he allowed himself to believe they had a chance, and it fell apart . . .

It would be devastating.

He didn't have to take that chance. What he had with Connor and Travis worked. And they had no problem with him knowing what aroused them, especially when he acted on it.

Gazing at Lindsay's beaming face, he did not want to ruin what they had left of this weekend. She was beautiful and happy. Sexy and wild. He didn't want to lose a minute of that during this fantasy weekend. Then, when it was over tomorrow, he would say good-bye to her forever. Because if he didn't, he'd be tempted to be an idiot and risk his heart.

He cuddled her close and she sighed, her soft breath tickling his chest.

"Don't you have to take that wet thing off?" she asked, stroking down his stomach toward his limp cock. She toyed with the base of him and he knew, very soon, she'd have him hard again.

He sat up and pulled the condom off, then wrapped it in a tissue and set it on the side table.

He arched his eyebrow. "Is there a reason you want my cock naked again?"

She wrapped her hand around it, and it twitched at the feel of her soft, delicate fingers. Then with a firm grip she began stroking.

"I just want to see how many times I can keep you going. Unless you'd like me to call the other guys in. Maybe the three of you could put on a little show for me. You know, you suck Connor while Travis fucks Connor and sucks you."

He grinned. "I'm not sure if that would work. Position-wise, I mean."

"Hmm. If you lie down and . . ." She curled her body as if trying to work it out, then shrugged and sat up. "Well, I'm sure you'd work out something supremely erotic for me to watch."

He stroked her hair from her face. "You really have no problem with the relationship between Connor, Travis, and me."

She shrugged. "Why would I?" She grinned. "Especially when it's so intensely sexy."

He chuckled. "I'll tell you what's intensely sexy." He grabbed her shoulders and pressed her onto her back, then grabbed her thighs and tugged her to the bottom of the bed. "You."

He knelt on the floor, pulling her lower until her legs draped over the end, then he pressed them wide and licked her slit. She was slick and warm, and tasted a little salty. And sweet.

He drove his tongue into her opening and she moaned. He glided his thumbs along her folds, then opened them until he could see her clit in the little nest of pink skin. He dabbed it with his tongue and she inhaled sharply.

He licked and kissed until she arched against him. He suckled lightly.

"Oh, God, I'm going to . . ." she moaned.

His heart rate accelerated knowing he was bringing her such intense pleasure. Her fingers glided through his short hair and she pulled him tighter against her. He obliged, sucking deeper while gliding two fingers into her slick opening.

"Oh, yeah . . ." She tightened her fingers around his head. "Oh, God."

Then she wailed loud and long. He had no doubt Connor and Travis could both hear her. And were probably jealous as all get out. His own cock throbbed at the exquisite sound.

When she finally collapsed against the bed, she groaned and opened her arms to him.

"Oh, God, fuck me now. Please, for God's sake fuck me."

He laughed, then slid her up the bed and prowled over her, then drove deep. She gasped, wrapping her arms around him. He thrust and thrust. She immediately started to wail again and he felt his balls tighten.

"Oh, shit." Damn it, he didn't have a condom on. He pulled out of her hot, wet body just in time to spray all over her flat stomach.

He groaned as he finished ejaculating, the cool air a shock to his poor, excited cock. When the spurting stopped, he rolled onto his back beside her.

"I'm sorry about that." He grabbed a tissue and wiped the white liquid from her skin.

"Are you, um . . . I mean, have you been tested recently?" she asked.

"Yes, of course. I made sure . . . we all made sure . . . before we invited you to this weekend."

"But you didn't tell me."

"Well, none of us felt it was reasonable to expect you to give us that level of trust. I mean, you didn't know us. We wouldn't ask you to trust us so completely as to put your life, or your health, at risk."

She smiled. "But you did ask me to trust you enough to have sex with you."

"Safe, protected sex. But we got tested anyway, to be completely sure."

She nodded. "I've been tested recently, too. And I'm on birth control. So why don't we forget about the condoms from now on?"

"That's great with me. But I'm curious. Why did you get tested? I mean, you said you didn't believe this was really a fantasy weekend. You thought your friend had set it up as a girls' getaway."

"I know. It wasn't because of that. It was because . . . a couple of weeks before I ran into you guys in the elevator, I had broken up with my boyfriend."

"So we're rebound sex?" He grinned.

She shrugged, but her sour expression prompted him to ask more rather than let it die with a lame joke.

"So what happened?"

"I caught him with two other women."

"He sounds like a jerk."

She nodded. "After that, I figured I should be tested. Who knows how many others he'd been with or how careful he'd been?" She glanced at him. "But the tests came back clean, so you don't have anything to worry about."

He smiled, then stroked her cheek. "I know. I trust you." He leaned in and brushed his lips against hers in a light kiss. "He really was a jerk, you know." He grazed his thumb across her cheek in a gentle caress. "To do anything so stupid to endanger his relationship with you. He was a grade-A, king-sized jerk."

That's why she'd had such trouble accepting his statement that she was special when they were at the restaurant.

Because her stupid ex-boyfriend had killed her sense of self-worth. He'd love to find the guy and pound him out.

Not that he'd do that. Very bad behavior for a cop.

She curled her arms around him and leaned against his chest. He held her close, enjoying her softness in his arms. Then he started when he felt dampness against his chest and realized it was her tears. He tightened his arms around her.

"Lindsay? You okay?"

She nodded. "I just . . ." She sucked in a breath. "I just didn't really let myself think about it until now, but . . ." She drew in another breath and snuffled a little. He handed her a tissue from the box at the side of the bed, then drew her close again while she dabbed at her eyes. "You know, it's just that it hurt . . . what he did."

He stroked her hair. "Of course it did. It was a terrible betrayal."

She snuffled, then blew her nose again. "It's not even the other women. I mean, that made me mad, he was a jerk, but . . . he said I was boring."

"Is that why you decided to stay this weekend? To prove you're not boring?"

"Well, partly, yes. But not to prove it to him. I needed to prove it to myself."

Erik pulled Lindsay on top of him, her soft breasts cushioned against his hard chest. "How can a woman who has hot, uninhibited sex with three men believe—in any way, shape, or form—that she's boring?"

She giggled and sat up, her hot pussy on top of his

150

cock. He loved seeing her face light up the way it was right now and, as she shifted her body on his pelvis, his cock began to swell. Man, he'd really thought he was done for the night. With this woman, however . . . with Lindsay . . . he never seemed to lose interest. Or have his fill.

But he'd better get his fill, because tomorrow it ended.

She wrapped her hand around his swollen cock and pressed it to her, then he glided inside. Oh, sweet heaven, she felt good around him. She moved up and down on him, stroking her breasts, then she swiveled her hips, causing his cock to swirl inside her slick passage with a mind-blowing caress of sensations. Then she began to ride him in earnest, her breathing coming in pants as she pounded up and down on him. Pleasure swamped his senses. His groin ached and his balls tightened. As soon as she tossed back her head and moaned, her face alight with an ecstatic radiance, he erupted inside her with a groan.

She moved on him, his cock gliding deep inside her, her whimpers continuing. Then she slowed, and finally, slumped onto his chest.

She drew in a deep breath. "Mmm, I'm sleepy." She nuzzled his neck, then rested her head on his shoulder. "Can I sleep like this?"

He stroked her hair behind her ear, then left his hand on her head, cradling it against him. "Sure. Anything you want."

He nuzzled her ear. Soft wisps of golden hair tickled his face. After a few moments, her deep breathing told him she was asleep. His cock was still buried inside her warmth. He could feel her heartbeat against his. He felt so close to her. He felt . . . like he belonged. To her. And she belonged to him.

Ah, fuck. That's exactly what he didn't want.

Travis glanced up as Erik trod into the kitchen, yawning, wearing just his boxers and a robe hanging open.

"Hey, man, how are you doing?" Travis asked.

"He got to fuck Lindsay all night long." Connor grinned. "He's doing fucking great."

Yeah, hearing the noises of pleasure she made had driven Travis nuts. He'd wanted to be with her, too. At the sounds, Connor had jumped Travis and fucked him until they'd both collapsed in one another's arms. As great as that had been, Travis had wanted Lindsay in bed with them.

He handed Erik a mug of coffee, then sat across from him at the kitchen table.

Connor pushed aside his empty plate and stared at Erik. "You seem to be getting attached to our guest."

"That's right. Can you seriously walk away after to-day?" Travis sipped his coffee, hoping Erik would say no.

"No problem. You know my history with women. You know how devastated I was when Cyndi left. And the others. I don't need that."

"Why are you so sure Lindsay will do the same thing?"

"They all do."

"Lindsay's different," Travis said.

Erik's intense blue eyes speared Travis. "She's only here for the weekend. Today she leaves. That was the agreement. Everyone knew it coming in."

"Yeah, but that can change," Travis said.

Connor glanced at Travis. "Are you saying you want it to change?"

Of course he fucking wanted it to change. In her arms he felt complete. Wanted. He didn't want to lose that. But he couldn't just blurt that out.

"Well, she is the hottest woman ever to take on the three of us," he said instead.

"Yes, she is." Erik finished his coffee and set the mug down. "So let's enjoy today to the fullest."

When Lindsay came out of the shower, she found a tray of breakfast sitting on the table near the window. It contained breakfast for one. She was surprised that Erik wouldn't be eating with her.

Her cell phone chimed and she glanced around for her purse, then retrieved it from the dresser. She opened it and took out her phone.

Text me when you're done with breakfast. —Erik

She smiled and responded with "Ok."

She pulled out the chair and sat down. As she ate, she gazed at the view of the city outside the window. Why did he want her to text him? He probably had some kind of surprise planned. And from her experience so far this weekend, she could hardly wait to see what it was.

She took her last sip of coffee, then put down the cup and tapped out her message on the phone.

I'm done.

She stood up and gazed out the window at the sunny streets below and the people walking along the sidewalks and crossing at intersections. A small grin curled her lips. She must be special because none of those people had the extreme good fortune she had found this weekend, having three sensationally hunky men bringing her sexual fantasies to life.

A loud knock at the door startled her.

"Open the door." Erik's voice sounded loud and authoritative from the hallway.

"Coming." She hurried to the door, wondering if this was the start of a role-playing scenario or if something was wrong. But if something was wrong, surely he would come right in.

She opened the door and came face-to-face with a blue uniform stretched across a broad chest. A police uniform. Her gaze lifted to Erik's face, severe looking under his brimmed blue hat.

"Lindsay Reed?" Erik demanded.

"Uh . . . yes, sir."

He grasped her arm and drew it forward, then she felt the bite of cold steel against her wrist. "You are under arrest." The metal cuff snapped closed, then he took her other arm and secured that wrist with the other cuff.

Thirteen

Adrenaline raced through her. Oh, God, this was so sexy!

"Come with me." Erik led her down the hall and into the living room, then around to the bar against one wall.

She stared wide-eyed at Travis and Connor who were sitting on the couch watching. Travis winked at her.

"Sit," Erik barked.

She perched on the tall stool that had been turned to face the room.

"What is it, Officer? What did I do?"

"Don't play dumb with me. You know very well you broke into these gentlemen's apartment."

"But I was invited."

"To come in here when no one was home? That's breaking and entering. And the invitation? Totally bogus. You'll have to do better than that next time."

"What are you going to do with me?"

"Well, I should take you straight to jail, but the

gentlemen have decided not to press charges. On one condition."

She gazed at him, waiting. But he said no more, so she finally asked, "What condition?"

"That you make it up to them."

She glanced at Connor and Travis. "What do you want me to do?"

Connor leaned forward on the couch. "Come now."

She stared at him blankly. Of course she knew they were expecting some kind of sexual compensation, and the thought of playing out the role of sexual slave to these men excited her, but she thought they'd give her more direction than that.

Connor kept a serious expression. "I said, come. Now."

She stifled a giggle. Leave it to Connor to be so corny.

"Let me help." Erik leaned down and unfastened the belt at her waist, then peeled back her satiny robe, exposing . . . well, everything . . . to view.

She was totally naked beneath the robe. Her nipples hardened as the three men stared at her naked breasts. She heard the clank of chains and Erik crouched down. Cold metal snapped around her ankle, then he drew it to the side and back. Then he drew her other ankle back, spreading her naked thighs, and fastened a metal band around her ankle. When he released her, she realized the metal bands around her ankles were attached by a chain which he'd threaded around the back legs of the stool, so her legs were held apart.

Connor stared straight at her, his gaze locking right

between her spread thighs. Then his gaze shifted to her face and he smiled expectantly.

"Miss, have you decided not to cooperate," Erik asked, "because I can take you straight to jail if you'd prefer?"

"No, I don't want to go to jail."

"Then I think you'd better . . . *come*." Travis tried to stifle a grin but didn't succeed too well.

She glanced at the handcuffs holding her wrists together, but Erik . . . the police officer . . . made no move to unlock them. She brought her hands to her breasts and stroked, the chain clinking with her movements. She ran her fingers over her nipples until they ached from the stimulation. Oh, she'd love one of the men to hold her breasts in his big palms. She slid her hands down her belly to her thighs, then stroked between them. Her fingers found her folds and she opened them, then slid her finger inside. She was already wet.

Of course she was. A hot sexy cop had just arrested her and dragged her out here to be a sex slave to two other sexy men. All in the comfort of this luxurious penthouse. How could she not be turned on?

"Are you wet?" the police officer asked.

She nodded.

"Then show them."

She opened her folds to show the men her slickness. Then she slid a finger inside.

"Wait, I've changed my mind," Connor said. "I don't think she should come yet."

He leaned in to whisper something to Travis and Travis nodded his head.

"Officer," Travis said, "don't you think you're a little to blame that she got in here? Since you should have been patrolling?"

Erik narrowed his eyes and hesitated, then reluctantly said, "Yes, sir, I suppose you're right."

"All right then. We think you should make amends, too. Come over here, please."

Erik stepped toward the couch. The stool Lindsay was sitting on was angled so she had a perfect view of the two men sitting on the couch and the police officer standing in front of them. Connor unzipped his pants and reached inside, then drew out his long cock. It was hard and thick and dark red. Erik crouched in front of him and wrapped his hand around it, then swallowed the big cockhead into his mouth and sucked, then dove forward and back and few times.

"My turn." Travis took out his cock.

Erik released Connor, then grabbed Travis' already stiff cock. He wrapped his lips around the head and surged forward.

He shifted back and forth between the two cocks until both men were close to bursting. "Okay, that's enough," Connor said.

Erik stood up and Travis guided him across the room until he stood in front of Lindsay. Connor followed them.

Travis unzipped Erik, then wrapped his hand around his swollen cock and drew it free. Connor guided Lindsay's head downward toward Erik's cock. She leaned forward until the cock-head pressed against her lips.

"Suck it," Travis said.

She opened her lips and Travis fed the big, marble-hard cock into her mouth.

"Make him come," Connor said.

She swirled her tongue around him, feeling him twitch in her mouth. Travis continued to hold the big cock at the base and pushed it in and out of her mouth. She squeezed as it moved inside her, then began to suck. Erik groaned, then his body stiffened. A gush of hot liquid filled her mouth. She gagged a little as the big penis continued to drive in and out of her mouth under Travis' direction.

Connor nudged Travis' arm. "Hey, don't choke her."

"Oh, right. Sorry." Travis stopped the movement and drew Erik's cock free. She swallowed the salty liquid, but some spilled from her mouth.

Travis leaned down and licked the trickle along the side of her chin, then slid his tongue into her mouth and swirled inside. "Mmm. I've tasted him, now I want to taste her."

Travis knelt down in front of her, between her thighs, and gazed hungrily at her folds.

Connor grabbed a stool and placed it at an angle to hers. "Officer, why don't you sit here?"

As soon as he sat down, Connor pressed his cock to the police officer's face. Travis turned his head and watched with her as Erik wrapped his hands around the thick, hard cock and brought the head to his lips. Lindsay felt shivers as she watched the big male member slide into the police officer's mouth.

Then she jumped as something brushed her folds. She glanced down to see Travis slide his finger along her slit, then he leaned forward and licked her. Her gaze shifted back to Connor's cock disappearing and reappearing from the officer's mouth.

Travis licked her, then his tongue found her clit and he swirled it around. Her fingers curled in his long hair. As the pleasure rose, she slumped on the stool. Connor groaned as the police officer sucked on him. Travis sucked her and his fingers slipped into her opening, stroking her inside.

"Fuck, I'm coming." Connor arched his pelvis forward, then shuddered as the police officer sucked him to climax.

Intense sensations pulsed through her as Travis stroked, then suckled her delicate bud. An orgasm erupted inside her and she moaned her own release.

"God, now I want to fuck someone." Travis stood up and guided her head down to his cock, then pushed inside her mouth.

She opened her throat, allowing him deep access. He glided in a couple of times, then slid free. He forked his fingers through her long hair and gently drew her head back, then pressed his balls to her mouth. She licked them.

"Open your mouth. Wide."

She did as he said and he reached underneath and guided

his clean-shaven balls into her mouth. She sucked a little, pulling them farther, then she gently massaged, puckering her mouth and gliding her tongue over them.

"Oh, yeah." He drew them out, then pushed his cockhead to her lips again and glided inside.

After several strokes, he backed away, then walked to Connor and turned him to face the back of the couch perpendicular to the one they'd sat on before. Connor dropped his pants and stripped away his boxers. Then he leaned forward, his hands resting on the back of the couch. Excitement skittered through her as she watched Travis' big cock disappear into Connor's ass.

Erik stepped behind her, then crouched down, watching them over her shoulder. His hands found her breasts and he massaged them while they watched Travis fuck Connor. His big cock gliding in and out. Connor groaned, his own cock so stiff she was sure he would explode at any moment. Travis thrust faster, his hands firmly holding Connor's hips. Connor groaned, then white, foamy liquid squirted from his cock. Travis groaned, too, continuing to thrust and thrust.

One of Erik's hands drifted down and found her clit, then stroked it, while he nuzzled the base of her neck. She turned her head to look at him, and saw the police hat on his head.

Excitement quivered through her again. He was the police officer. And he was touching her.

Connor and Travis turned and gazed her way, then they smiled and walked toward her.

"I think it's time you pay your debt to society." Connor grinned. "And by society, I mean the three of us."

Connor grasped her arms and urged her to stand. Her legs were still attached to the stool so she could do no more than stand there, her legs wide apart, with the tall stool between her legs. Erik moved in front of her, his big cock protruding from his dark, blue uniform. He positioned himself between her legs and pressed his big cock-head to her slick opening.

Oh, God, he was an officer of the law and he was about to fuck her.

He drove forward with authority. He glided in several times, sending her hormones skyrocketing, then he pulled free. With disappointment she sucked in a breath as he disappeared behind her.

Connor stepped forward and his cock-head nudged her opening. He was only semi-rigid but he pushed inside her. Then Travis, also with a partially revived erection, stepped in close, too. To her surprise, he nudged his cock-head against her already full opening, and slid inside next to Connor.

Oh, God, she had two cocks inside her. Both in her vagina. She couldn't believe it. And they were growing.

"This is a tight squeeze, but . . . fuck! . . . it feels good." Connor pushed forward and his steadily growing cock filled her deeper.

Travis pushed in deeper, too. But the growing cocks stretched her tightly.

"Is it too much, Lindsay?" Erik murmured against her ear.

"Um . . ." The cocks filled her tighter and tighter. "I think . . . maybe."

Immediately, Travis withdrew.

"Fuck, doll, you feel so good around me." Connor began to thrust into her.

He thrust fast and hard. Filling her. Taking her breath away. Pleasure flared. He groaned and thrust super deep. She moaned as his hot semen filled her, then he pulled out.

"Don't worry, sweet thing, you've got a spare cock right here." Travis drove into her, his cock impaling her fast and hard.

She grabbed a handful of his shirt, the cuffs preventing her from clinging to his shoulders. Her insides quivered and pleasure rose again. He groaned and filled her with hot liquid, then drew away.

"Oh, no," she wailed, hovering on the edge.

Now Erik stepped in front of her. He pressed his hot flesh to her opening, then drove inside. His cock filled her again and again and she spun off into a wild surge of pleasure. She sucked in a breath, then exploded into ecstasy. She wailed as the whole world seemed to fade away, except his hard thrusting shaft.

"Oh . . . God . . . yessss . . ." Her voice seemed far away as her body dissipated in a cloud of bliss.

———

Erik felt Lindsay slump against him. He wrapped his arm around her waist, then realized she was sliding downward.

"Man, you did it again," Connor said. "Do you always make the woman faint?"

"Only when I'm a police officer, it seems." He very distinctly remembered her calling him *Officer* the last time, and how much it had turned him on.

"Connor, get the key from my pocket and undo the cuffs on her ankles."

Travis helped Erik steady her so she didn't slide to the floor. Connor reached into Erik's pocket and his fiddling around looking for the key caused Erik's cock to lurch, but then Connor's hand withdrew and he freed Lindsay's ankles.

Erik scooped her up and carried her to the couch, then laid her down.

"I'll get some water," Travis said.

Erik knelt beside the couch and watched her face. Last time she'd fainted, she'd woken up pretty quickly. Travis placed a glass of water on the side table just as her eyelids flickered open. She gazed at Erik and smiled.

"Officer, am I free to go?"

Oh, God, she was so beautiful. Her face still glowed from the pleasure they'd given her. He hadn't finished and his erection throbbed with need. His gaze traveled down her body, then fell on her naked breasts. The nipples puckered. God, she was turned on just by him looking at her.

"Not quite yet, ma'am." He had to touch her, so he stroked over her bare breast, then cupped it. The nipple pushed into his palm.

"Officer, are you going to fuck me?"

He prowled over her on the couch.

"That's exactly what I'm going to do." He nudged his cock-head against her folds.

"Oh, you can't do that." But she opened her legs to him.

He chuckled, then thrust deep. Oh, God, it was heaven to be inside her like this. His cock was cradled in her soft, womanly passage.

Then she squeezed him and he groaned.

He drew back and thrust forward again. Then again.

"Oh, yes. Fuck me." She arched against him, taking him so deep he thought he'd disappear into her sweetness. "Fuck me hard."

He drew back and jerked forward, burying himself even deeper, then thrust again. His rhythm increased until he was drilling into her in a blur of movement, their bodies slapping together, her moans increasing.

Then she clung to him, wailing. He kept pumping until his balls tingled, then hot liquid erupted from him. Holding her body tightly to his, he groaned as he released inside her.

Finally, he slumped against her, being careful to hold some of his weight on his knees and elbows. He glanced down at her, smiling, only to see her eyes were closed.

"Not again." He was flattered beyond belief that he

could send her spinning into unconsciousness from sheer pleasure, but too much didn't seem like a good thing.

She opened one eye and stared up at him, then giggled. "It's okay. I'm just resting."

His heart fluttered and he laughed. God, this woman was a total delight.

And this was his last day with her.

He captured her lips and kissed her, his tongue diving into her mouth to sweep possessively inside. Damn it, he didn't want to lose her. He wanted her to stay here forever with him.

Which was exactly why she had to go. Today. Now.

But he couldn't bear to lose her right now. It would be hard enough later. Right now, he wanted to enjoy every last minute with her.

The afternoon and evening slipped away, far too fast for Lindsay's liking. Before she knew it, it was dark outside and she was in bed wrapped in Travis' big arms, with Connor in front of her, her cheek resting against his solid back. After a wild round of rousing sex between the four of them, Erik had slipped away while she snuggled with Travis and Connor.

Sadly, she knew she'd have to pull herself away soon and head home.

"Hey, there, it's almost nine o'clock."

She glanced around to see Erik standing in the doorway, lit from behind by the hall light. The bedroom was lit by a single lamp on the bedside table. Connor muttered, then sat up, settling his feet on the floor. He stood up and grabbed his clothes from the chair and began pulling them on. Travis kissed the back of her neck and slipped away from her. She missed their warmth immediately. She rolled onto her back and pushed herself up on the pillows, watching the two men dress.

Erik continued to stare at her with an unsettling intensity. Travis glanced at Erik, then at her. He grabbed Connor's arm, then led him from the room.

She sat up. "I guess I should be getting ready to go."

He stepped into the room and closed the door behind him. "Not yet."

Fourteen

As Lindsay moved closer, Erik could see the heat darkening his deep blue eyes. He pulled off his T-shirt as he stepped closer, then unfastened his jeans. She felt a thrill quiver through her as he pushed them down. A second later, he pushed off his boxers, too, and she was facing a humongous hard-on. It was big and bulging, and it began to twitch at her intense stare.

"See something you like?" he asked, a gleam in his eye.

She dragged her gaze to his face, then slowly down his sensational, muscle-bound body. "I like everything I see."

He chuckled, then pulled back the covers and glided in beside her. He took her lips in a passionate kiss, drawing her tight to his naked body. Hot, hard flesh pressed the length of her, and his solid erection pressed tight against her stomach. She was still slick from the last round of intense sex with the three of them, so he could slide right in with no problem. But from the gentle persuasion of his lips, and the way his tongue lightly cajoled hers, she could tell he wanted slow and intimate. She could almost feel his desire for her to touch him gently and tenderly. In fact, the feeling was so compelling it pulsed through her with an overwhelming intensity. It must just be her imagination, but she pressed her hand to his chest and eased him onto his back, then climbed over him, intent on fulfilling that need.

"Sweetheart, I want to go slow—"

She captured his lips, stilling his words. "I know."

She kissed him again, gently, then nipped his lips and outlined his mouth with the tip of her tongue. He pulled her tight, pressing his tongue deep. She sucked lightly, then her lips slipped from his. Shooting him a quick grin, she pressed her lips to his neck and nuzzled, then glided down his solid chest to his nipple. The little nub was hard as a bead as she took it in her mouth, then she sucked. He groaned, his hand cupping her head and stroking.

She pinched his nipple between her fingertips as she kissed across his chest. She stroked and teased his hard nub as she covered the other with her mouth and teased it with her tongue, then sucked, eliciting another groan from him.

She pushed herself up and sat on his hips, the bulge of his big cock lying on his stomach and cradled against her slick folds. It was difficult not to squirm and shimmy on that delightfully big, hard column beneath her, but she sat still and stroked over his shoulders and chest, then down his tight abs to his navel, avoiding his lovely cock-head, then back up again. She stroked him, round and round, teasing his nipples as she glided over them.

He arched against her hands and she leaned forward and lapped at one hard nub, then sucked again. Suddenly, she felt a deep need for his mouth on her pussy, his tongue diving into her wet opening, then curling over her clit. It was so sudden and intense, she almost dropped to the bed and flung open her legs in desperate invitation.

Erik grasped her shoulders. "I want to taste you. Right now." The need burned in his eyes. It was almost as if he were reading her mind. No, actually, as if she'd been reading his.

He rolled her onto her back and prowled over her, then lifted her knees and licked her belly. Then he moved lower. He gave her a big smile, then dove in. She gasped as his tongue flicked her clit, then he licked the length of her sopping slit. He licked several times, then drove his tongue in deep. She could feel it swirl within her. A moment later, he covered her clit and teased mercilessly. Pleasure flickered through her, rising and falling as he manipulated her clit with practiced expertise.

She arched against his mouth, her fingers curling around his head. Right at this moment she felt so close to him. So cared for by him. His tongue flicked again.

"Oh, Erik, that feels so good."

He gazed up at her, his eyes gleaming with emotion. A feeling of tenderness washed through her with overwhelming intensity. She couldn't help wondering if it was his or hers. Which made no sense. How could she be feeling what he felt?

Her gaze locked with his and for a moment she wanted to say something. To tell him how much she needed him. To say how much she wanted him in her life.

Then he flicked his tongue and all thought dashed from her brain. Another flick and pleasure swamped her senses. When she arched and he suckled her button, blissful sensations exploded within her and she moaned.

Still he cajoled her nub, pushing her higher and higher until she wailed in complete abandon. She hung in the abyss of pure pleasure, then slowly fluttered back to Earth, but a need swelled within her.

She opened her arms. "Erik, make love to me."

His gaze locked on her face, his expression solemn. He prowled upward, his big muscular body moving over hers. She stroked down his chiseled chest, then his sculpted abs, and found his granite-hard cock. It twitched as she wrapped her hand around it. Pressing it to her smoldering wet opening, she gazed deep into his midnight-blue eyes.

"I want you," she said.

He cupped her cheeks. "Oh, God, Lindsay, I want you, too."

His lips claimed hers with a hard, demanding passion that took her breath away. Then he drove forward, his big, hard cock filling her completely.

She gasped. "Oh, Erik, yes."

He captured her lips in a quick but compelling kiss,

then nuzzled her neck. "God, I love it when you say my name while I'm giving you pleasure."

He drew back and drove deep again, his big cock gliding along her inner passage. She gasped and clung to him. He drew back and thrust again, seeming to go deeper still. She squeezed him and he groaned.

"Oh, God, Lindsay, that feels so good."

Her name on his lips sent tingles through her. It made her feel special and . . . loved.

He stroked loose tendrils of hair from her face and gazed at her. The need in the depths of his glittering eyes rocked her.

He thrust again and she clutched him to her body, emotions swirling with the wild sensations coiling through her.

"I want to make you come so hard, you'll never forget this time with me." He covered her lips and kissed her while he thrust again.

She arched against him. His tongue slid into her mouth and she sucked it deep. Pleasure swelled within her. He drew his face away and watched her as he plunged into her again and again, his huge cock filling her with bliss.

The sensations bombarded her, flinging her close to the edge.

"Oh, God, Erik. You're"—Lindsay sucked in a breath— "making me come." She tightened her arms around him as bliss surged through her. "Erik." His name slipped from her lips, then she sucked in a breath and wailed as the orgasm exploded within her. It filled her body and her soul, launching her to a place of pure wonder.

Afterward, she lay in his arms, reveling in the hard plains of his body close to hers and his big arms holding her protectively. She felt complete and utter contentment.

"Lindsay."

She opened her eyes at Erik's gentle urging.

"It's getting late."

A quick glance at the clock on the bedside table told her she'd dozed off. It was almost ten.

"Oh, right. I need to be getting home." She had work in the morning.

He didn't protest as she pushed the covers aside and stood up. Erik got dressed quickly while she gathered her clothes.

"I'll leave you to finish packing." Erik left the room, closing the door behind him.

After she took a quick shower in the en suite and dressed, she picked up her toiletries bag, then went to the guest room down the hall where her suitcase was. She packed up the few clothes she'd put in the dresser, then grabbed her purple purse and the overnight bag and carried them into the living room.

All three men were waiting for her and stood up. Travis took her bags from her hand and Connor gave her a big hug. Travis put down her bags and tugged her into his arms for a sound kiss. Although she loved being in their now-familiar arms, this felt too much like a good-bye, and surely after what they'd shared—and what she and Erik had shared—she would be seeing them again.

Travis released her and she turned to face Erik. He stepped forward and gave her a quick hug. When he released her, she gazed up at him with a smile.

"Lindsay, we're really glad you decided to stay the weekend, especially after the misunderstanding about the invitation."

"Me, too." She smiled. "But how could I resist a date with a handsome police officer, then a chance to share some *good times* with his sexy friends."

He stroked her cheek. "I'll miss you."

"Miss me?" Her stomach fluttered. "You mean . . . I won't be seeing you again?"

Erik's lips compressed. "I'm sorry, I thought you understood. The invitation was just for the weekend."

Her heart thumped loudly in her chest. "But I didn't accept the invitation to a fantasy sex weekend. I accepted an invitation for a date with you. I thought . . . I mean, we seemed to connect so well. I thought we would keep seeing each other."

Erik shook his head. "I'm afraid not."

Her stomach clenched. This couldn't be happening. With all that had happened between them, with the way he'd looked at her, the way he'd touched her . . . she'd been sure he had felt something special between them, too.

She glanced at Connor, but he avoided her gaze. Travis stared at his feet, his head shaking.

"Come on. I'll drive you home," Erik said.

Connor picked up her overnight bag, and he and Travis followed them to the elevator. They rode in silence, and Connor and Travis gave her warm hugs before she climbed into the car.

Shock tingled through her as she directed Erik to her place, then he pulled up at the front entrance of her building.

She shook her head and gazed at his expressionless face.

"Just tell me why?" The words slipped from her lips before she could stop them.

He shrugged. "I'm already in a relationship."

The blood in her veins turned to ice. "You are?" Had he been cheating on a girlfriend this weekend? Just like Glen had cheated on her?

"With Travis and Connor."

"Oh, well, they seemed to enjoy having me." Her cheeks flushed a little at the wording, but she forged on. "Couldn't we continue the way we were this weekend, with all three of us?"

"So you'd be dating three guys at the same time?"

She smiled. "Sounds pretty good to me."

He sighed, and the hope that had been building in her dissipated.

"Connor, Travis, and I have known each other for a long time. Although I'm fine having the odd woman join us for a short time, what we three men have together works. Adding a female element for a longer term changes the dynamic." He gazed at her with unsettling intensity.

"Lindsay, you're a beautiful, vibrant, sexy woman. But my commitment is to Connor and Travis, and I don't want to endanger that."

She wanted to protest—to convince him it would work—but instead she pushed her shoulders back and reached for the door. "Okay." She pushed it open and climbed out of the car.

Erik hopped out of the car and grabbed her overnight bag from the back. "I'll carry this up for you."

"That's okay. I can manage." She took it from his hand, careful not to touch him. She did not want to feel that electrical attraction. Then she turned and headed for the door.

Erik's heart ached as he watched her walk away. The flicker of rejection in her eyes had nearly been his undoing, but he had made his choice long before she came along. He did not want a woman in his life. Sure, they'd experienced a strong connection, and he could understand why she might expect him to suggest they continue seeing each other, but specifically because of that connection, he couldn't chance it. If he allowed it to build, then the pain of losing her would be even more devastating than it had been with Cyndi.

And if he lost her, and Connor and Travis were even more attached to her than they had been to Becci, who had almost torn the three of them apart, then he was in real danger of losing the two of them, too. His relationship

177

with Travis and Connor was everything to him. He wouldn't risk that for a woman, no matter how strong the attraction.

Still, he drank in the sight of her until the glass doors closed behind her and she disappeared around a corner. Then he started the car and drove away.

Erik woke up with a huge hard-on. He'd been dreaming of Lindsay. Her lips around his cock. Coming in her mouth. Then her gliding into his arms and kissing him until uncontrollable passion flared and he made love to her until she wailed his name in ecstasy.

Fuck, he could deal with that, but it was the gnawing need to have her in his arms, to see her sweet face on his pillow and the glow in her eyes when she gazed at him that had his gut tied in knots.

He'd spent half the night tossing and turning, the image of Lindsay's forlorn expression in the elevator haunting him.

Damn it, now he was lying here, hot and hungry for her, and getting more depressed by the minute. What a lousy way to start a week.

He wrapped his hand around his erection, deciding to take care of his physical need, then realized there was another option.

Fifteen

Naked, Erik pushed himself from the bed and wandered out the door and down the hall, then tapped on Travis' door.

"Huh?" came the raspy reply from behind the door.

"Travis, it's me. Erik."

"Yeah, come in," Travis said in a sleep-roughened voice.

Erik opened the door and stepped inside.

"What's up?" Travis asked, then saw Erik's stiff cock. "Ah, that's what. Need a little help?"

"I was hoping." Erik crossed the room and climbed into bed.

Travis pushed himself to his knees, then wrapped his hand around Erik's cock. "Been dreaming about me?"

Erik chuckled. "You know it." Then he sucked in a breath as Travis' lips surrounded his shaft.

Travis tongued his cock-head, licking it all over, then

under the ridge. He sucked a little, then glided deeper. It was so hot and tight in Travis' mouth, and Erik was already so turned on by his dreams, he knew he wouldn't last long.

"Fuck, man, that feels so good." Erik tucked his hands behind his head as Travis worked on him.

Travis cupped his balls and sucked hard, then bobbed up and down. Damn, it felt so good being touched by Travis. Heat steamed through him from his dreams, then boiled to a rising frenzy. Erik stiffened as he felt his balls tighten. Travis moved faster and Erik suddenly shot straight down his throat. Travis sucked and swallowed several times as Erik rode his climax.

Finally, he lay sprawled on the bed as Travis sat up. He plumped the pillows and sat stretched out beside Erik.

Erik sighed deeply, enjoying the dissipating pleasure, then pushed himself to his knees and grabbed Travis' cock, which had risen to full attention. It filled his hand with its girth. He stroked a couple of times, admiring the length of it. The way the veins pulsed along the shaft. Then he leaned forward and licked the tip, then swallowed the big cock-head. The hard, hot flesh in his mouth felt incredibly erotic. He squeezed it, pleased at Travis' moan. He glided down, taking it as deep as he could, at the same time stroking his balls.

He bobbed up and down, glancing up occasionally to see the rapt look on his friend's face. He glided off and sucked his balls, teasing them with his tongue, then he returned to sucking his cock.

Travis began to arch forward, filling Erik's mouth with cock. He continued thrusting while Erik sucked, and stroked his balls in the palm of his hand.

"Oh, God damn." Travis thrust again and hot liquid filled Erik's mouth.

He swallowed and sucked until Travis stopped spurting and collapsed on the bed. Erik stretched out beside him. His eyes closed and he felt fully relaxed for the first time since he went to bed last night. Why hadn't he thought of seeking out Travis or Connor earlier?

"Hey, Erik, you have to leave for work soon."

Erik's eyelids snapped open. A quick glance at the bedside clock and he realized he'd dozed off.

"Don't worry about breakfast. Connor's already up and making it."

"Great. I'll go grab a shower." Erik pushed himself from the bed and headed toward his bedroom.

"How about I join you?" Travis followed him.

As Travis slipped into the large tiled shower with him, Erik wondered what was up. Travis didn't usually do the shower-together thing.

Travis followed Erik into the shower, steeling himself for the conversation to come, but knowing he had to broach the topic.

"So, I wanted to talk to you about Lindsay."

"What about her?" Erik turned the water on.

"Well, it's clear you two had a thing going on between

you." Travis had actually been encouraged by the fact. He really believed Lindsay could be the one to help Erik get past his issues with women.

"We all had a thing going on with her." Erik stepped under the steaming water.

Travis picked up the soap and started scrubbing Erik's back.

"Sure, but there was a real chemistry between the two of you. It was clear you were fighting it, but it was there."

Erik shrugged. "Chemistry is overrated."

"Erik, I know you're gun-shy where women are concerned, and that you don't want another incident like with Becci, but I really think Lindsay is different. I think you should give her another chance and—"

Erik spun around and lightly shoved Travis against the tiled wall, then covered his mouth with his, driving his tongue deep inside. The powerful thrusts of Erik's tongue as he held him tight against the wall made Travis melt. He wanted to push back—to straighten things out about Lindsay—but, damn, he could never resist Erik as an authoritative cop.

Erik leaned against him, their wet, hard chests pressed tight against each other. Erik swirled his tongue in Travis' mouth until Travis' breathing turned deep and erratic, his groin tightening with need. Erik's hand glided down Travis' hip and between their bodies until he found Travis' rising cock and grasped it, his big fingers firm around him.

He pumped as he drew his face away. "I don't need a woman to keep me happy."

Travis stared at Erik's intense blue eyes, his own eyelids at half-mast. Erik chuckled. They both knew if Erik wanted to shut Travis up, all he had to do was step into the dominant role. Erik grabbed his shoulders and spun him around, then surged forward, pinning him to the wet, tiled wall. He grabbed the bottle of lube he kept on the inset shelf and smeared it on, then Travis felt the head of Erik's hard cock press against his ass. Erik slowly pressed forward, and Travis groaned as the broad head pushed into him. Erik eased inside until his shaft filled him.

"You like my big cock in your ass, Travis?" Erik coiled his fingers in Travis' long hair and tugged back, turning his face until they were eye to eye.

The intense hunger in Erik's eyes drove Travis' desire into high gear.

"Fuck, yeah," Travis groaned.

"Good. I do, too. Now shut up while I fuck you."

Erik released his hair and Travis leaned his face against the smooth wall as Erik drew back, then thrust deep into his tight ass. Travis moaned as Erik thrust again and again. Erik's groans of pleasure spiraled through Travis, driving his own pleasure higher. Suddenly, Erik's cock exploded inside Travis. That triggered Travis' own eruption. Erik jerked into him until his cock was totally spent, then he collapsed against him.

As Erik leaned back, his cock slipped free.

"Well, that was fun." Travis turned around and stepped under the water. As always, he'd enjoyed the sex with Erik, especially the part where he became the big, bossy cop, but disappointment surged through him that Erik had decided to avoid the Lindsay conversation.

He grabbed the shampoo and squeezed out a little, then began lathering up. "So I'm getting the message that you won't reconsider the situation with Lindsay."

Erik nodded approvingly. "Good."

Travis sipped his coffee. Breakfast between the three of them had been quieter than usual.

Erik stood up and placed his dishes by the sink. "I've got to get going."

Travis watched Erik, so sexy in his full uniform, walk through the kitchen doorway. Not only did Travis enjoy the physical relationship with Erik, he also admired him deeply. How many people would continue working, especially in such a dangerous career, once they inherited as much money as Erik had from his dad? Erik could easily retire, but he felt he was doing something important with his life and didn't want to give that up.

"So what the hell is going on between you two?"

Travis glanced at Connor, sitting across the table from him.

"I broached the subject of Lindsay with him this morning."

"I take it you didn't get very far with that."

Travis shook his head.

Since Erik had been so adamant about it, Travis didn't feel he had a choice but to drop it. He wanted to see Lindsay, but this was Erik's place and even though Erik had insisted that it was their home, too, Travis couldn't bring Lindsay here if Erik didn't agree to it. And he didn't.

"Did you tell him how important it is to you?"

Travis stood up and placed his cup by the sink, then opened the dishwasher to start loading the dishes. "I didn't really get into it."

"He pulled the dominant cop routine, right?"

Memories of being pressed against the tile wall by Erik's hard body sent quivers through him.

"He does it so well."

"Sure, but that doesn't mean he should ignore your needs."

Travis grinned. "Oh, he satisfied my needs."

"Travis, I'm serious. If he doesn't want to have a relationship with Lindsay, that's his choice, but there's no reason you and I shouldn't keep seeing her."

"You want to keep seeing her, too?"

"Hell, yeah."

Travis shook his head. "I don't like the idea of leaving Erik out. Especially after what happened with Becci."

"Becci was a totally different situation, and we're not leaving Erik out. You asked him and he declined. That's his decision, but he doesn't get to decide what you and I do." His eyes narrowed. "I'm assuming you'd like to pursue a relationship with Lindsay *and* me."

Travis saw the anxiety in Connor's eyes. He was the type of guy who didn't seem fazed by anything, but Travis could read him, and he was definitely worried.

"*If* I pursued a relationship with Lindsay, I would *love* for it to work out with the three of us." Travis was pleased to see the tension in Connor dissipate. "But as long as Erik's against it, I don't think it's a good idea."

Connor leaned forward, his intense gaze locked on Travis. "You told me that the way you feel about Lindsay is different than you've ever felt for a woman. Is that still true?"

Travis hesitated, but finally nodded.

"Okay, that's all I need to know."

The elevator doors opened and Erik walked into the penthouse, greeted by the delicious aroma of dinner. Smelled like stew. Connor's specialty.

Erik kicked off his shoes, then strolled into the living room and settled on the couch. It had been a long stressful day at work and all he wanted to do right now was unwind. Part of him wanted to head out to the pool for a swim, but it was just too much effort.

"Hey, you're home." Travis appeared from the hall and sat on the chair across from the couch.

"How's it going setting up the office?" Erik asked.

"Well, I have the wireless router connected to the Internet gateway now and all four computers are communicating through the local network. For the past hour,

I've been talking to tech support about the problems we had connecting the network drive and I think I've got what I need to get that going. Now my brain's fried and I need a break." He put his feet up on the wooden coffee table. "You look tired."

"Yeah, no kidding."

"I hope you two aren't too tired to enjoy the dinner I made." Connor popped his head out from the kitchen. "I've been slaving over the stove for hours."

"He has, too. I was tempted to chain him to the stove."

"Well, we still could. I've got my cuffs with me." Erik toyed with the leather handcuff case on his belt.

"Let's wait until after dinner, when he's done the dishes."

"I cooked, so it's your turn to do dishes," Connor protested.

Erik just chuckled. Connor and Travis shared the chores around the house. Erik tried to insist on taking a share, but Connor convinced him that Travis needed the arrangement to feel he was contributing enough to the household, since Erik wouldn't let them pay rent.

"But you wanted the development environment ready to go by tomorrow."

"Yeah, okay, I'll do them. But no chains." Connor disappeared into the kitchen.

"He says that now, but I'm sure we could convince him otherwise." Travis stood up. "You want a beer?"

"Sure."

Travis appeared a moment later with two beers and

handed one to Erik. He took a deep swig, enjoying the cold liquid in this throat.

Connor appeared with a bottle in his hand. "Dinner in forty-five minutes." He slumped onto the easy chair beside Travis. "How was your day, Erik?"

"Long. But I got a text from Cheryl today. I called her after my shift and she invited me to this thing on Friday."

Cheryl had been a woman the three of them had shared a nice, casual weekend with and she periodically called for a date with one or more of them.

"Yeah, she called here and I told her she should ask you. I figured it would help distract you from your Lindsay withdrawal."

Erik frowned. None of them had discussed Lindsay since Travis had brought it up in the shower over a week ago and he had hoped it would continue that way.

Connor grinned. "Knowing Cheryl, this 'thing' will keep you out until Saturday, or even Sunday."

"Cheryl's the one who loves threesomes, right?" Travis asked.

"Right. With two women," Connor answered.

"Sweet."

"She invited me to a birthday bash for a friend of hers who's turning thirty," Erik said.

Connor sipped his beer. "And she'll invite one of her girlfriends to join the two of you at her place afterward."

"And you will be the filling in a very sexy sandwich," Travis added.

Connor laughed. "Yeah, he'll be filling them all right."

Images of Cheryl and another woman stripping naked in front of him fluttered through Erik's mind. He wasn't sure if it was his fantasy or one of Travis' or Connor's. No matter. Connor was right, that would be how the evening would end. And it would be a great way to distract him from thoughts of Lindsay. Hell, probably all he needed was to get laid.

The phone on Lindsay's desk rang and she picked it up.

"Ms. Reed, this is reception. There's someone here to see you."

"I'm not expecting anyone. Who is it?"

"It's a Mr. Connor Jackson."

Her heart skipped a beat. "I'll be right down."

She hung up, grabbed her purse, and headed for the door. Was Travis with him?

And Erik?

As she rode down the elevator, her pulse quickened. It had been almost two weeks since the fabulous weekend she'd spent with the men and every night she fantasized about it. She missed them.

And she longed to see Erik again.

But she was a fool to think he was here with Connor. He'd made it very clear they were done. That she had just been a weekend fling.

Unless he'd changed his mind.

189

Sixteen

Lindsay glanced toward the receptionist's desk and saw Connor standing tall and looking sexier than any man had a right to. But just Connor.

He glanced her way and a broad smile claimed his face. He stepped toward her.

"Hey, there you are. I was in the neighborhood and thought you'd like to go to lunch."

"I would love to."

Her lips turned up in a wide smile. Maybe Erik wasn't here, but it was wonderful seeing Connor again. She was surprised that Travis wasn't with him, though. Why would Connor want to see her alone?

She walked with him to the entrance and he opened the door for her. Her body brushed his arm as she walked past him and excitement skittered along her nerve endings just being close to this sexy man again. They stepped from the air-conditioned office building into the heat of the bright, sunny day.

"My car's right over here." He pointed at a blue sedan by the curb.

"There are a lot of good restaurants right around here," she said as they walked along the sidewalk to his car.

"I'm sure there are, but I thought we might"—he winked as he opened the car door for her—"talk more freely at a restaurant where there won't be any of your coworkers."

She climbed into the car. Once they were inside she grinned. "So just what do you have in mind?"

"Just lunch, but as soon as I stop this car again, I plan to kiss the hell out of you." He started the engine and pulled into traffic.

She laughed, excitement skittering through her. God, after that unforgettable weekend, the past two weeks had been torturous. He glanced at her and grinned. "Hell, I'd like to do more than kiss you. Especially with you in your librarian suit."

She glanced down at her gray suit. It was more fitted than the one she'd worn for poker role-playing, and she wasn't wearing glasses, but she had her hair pinned up. Memories of that sexy session danced through her head and she wished she could spirit Connor away to her apartment and indulge in something more exciting than lunch.

Connor started the car and pulled into traffic.

"Where are we going?" she asked.

"There's a nice Italian place on Preston Avenue," he said, and five minutes later, they were walking into a quaint bistro and ordering from the lunch menu.

He filled her in on the launch they were planning for a cutting-edge game app, and the new technology it used. Lindsay was happy to see him so excited, but she kept wishing the conversation would turn to Erik. Seeing Connor delighted her, but it also made her miss the other guys.

"I really enjoyed seeing you today," she said when they got back in the car. "I've really missed that weekend we were all together."

"By the way, speaking of the infamous fantasy weekend . . ." Connor said.

"Yes?" Hope rose in her that he would say they'd missed her, too, and wanted to start seeing her again. Especially if Erik came as part of the package.

"You left these behind." Connor dug in his pocket and pulled out a pair of pink panties.

They were the ones she'd taken off during the poker game and Connor had put in his pants pocket.

"Travis told me they were obviously a match for the bra and garter belt, so I should return them."

She took the crumpled panties from Connor's outstretched hand. "Thanks. So that's why you came by." Not because he'd had an overwhelming need to see her.

"Well, it was a good excuse."

She glanced up at his beguiling grin. Warmth wafted through her. So he had wanted to see her.

"Listen. The other reason I came is because I wanted to tell you that Travis and I would really like to start seeing you again." He took her hand and kissed her knuckles. "So how about we pick you up for dinner after work on Friday?"

She smiled. "I'd like that."

Connor grinned. "And after that, you could come back to the penthouse."

Her heart rate quickened. "That would be great."

"And just in case you're worried about any awkwardness with Erik, he won't be there. He's got a date"—Connor winked—"and we don't expect him back until late the next day."

She felt like she'd been smacked in the face. That shattered any hope she'd had that Erik might want to see her again. Clearly, he wasn't missing her at all.

"Hopefully, the two of us can keep you entertained."

She nodded and smiled. "Of course."

She was being a fool. What did it matter if Erik didn't want to see her again? She was lucky two gorgeous men like Connor and Travis wanted to be with her.

"I guess I'd better get you back to work."

She glanced at the time display on her cell phone. She only had about fifteen minutes left of her lunch hour. Not that it mattered if she was a little late getting back, but if she stayed here any longer with this incredibly sexy man, she was likely to wind up in bed with him and not make it back to work at all.

———

Travis heard the hum of the elevator as he dried the last pot. Connor hadn't told him who he'd invited over tonight, just that it was a woman. Travis sighed. He would have preferred to skip it, but Connor really wanted this date tonight and Travis needed to consider Connor's needs, too.

No woman could compare to Lindsay, but maybe it would be good to be distracted from how much he was missing her. He dried his hands and then walked down the hall toward the opening doors of the elevator.

His eyes widened as he noticed Lindsay peering out at him. His heart leapt and he strode forward to meet her.

"Lindsay!"

She smiled and stepped out of the elevator, Connor on her heels.

"Travis, it's so nice to—"

He swept her into his arms and kissed her delicate lips. It was heaven having her soft body pressed to his again, feeling the sweet warmth of her mouth as his tongue glided inside. Her arms slid around him as she melted against him and he reveled in her closeness.

"Dinner smells good," Connor said from behind Lindsay.

Still holding her tight, he sent Connor a questioning look. Connor merely grinned at him. Travis mouthed Erik's name, and Connor shrugged.

"Let's open the wine," Connor said.

Travis released Lindsay and she placed her purple purse by the door and kicked off her sandals. For the first time, Travis noticed that Connor carried an overnight bag. He recognized it as the one Lindsay had brought to their weekend.

He beamed at her. "You're staying overnight?"

"I told her we had the place to ourselves until late tomorrow, so we'd love to have her."

Oh, God, yes. Travis wanted to have her. Right now. He captured her lips again, his groin tightening with need.

"You know, I can watch dinner if you two want to go and catch up," Connor said.

Dinner didn't need watching, since it was a casserole and would be in the oven for another hour. Connor knew that, too, but clearly wanted to give him some time alone with Lindsay. An opportunity he was thrilled to take advantage of.

"Would you like to go and catch up?" he asked, gazing into her eyes. He could see the heat in her twinkling blue eyes.

She stroked his cheek as she gazed up at him and nodded, a sweet smile curling her lips. He captured her hand and led her down the hall.

Seventeen

Lindsay loved the feel of Travis' big hands stroking her naked body tenderly, and the sweet brush of his lips on her skin. He'd wasted no time peeling the clothes from her body, then stripping off his own, and now they lay in bed together.

She ached with the need for him to glide inside her, but he seemed to want to explore every inch of her first. When his lips took her hard nipple, she arched against him. She wrapped her hand around his rock-hard cock and stroked. Oh, God, she wanted it.

She rolled onto her knees and pressed him onto his back, then kissed along his tight abs.

"But I want this to be for you," Travis said.

She grinned at him as she leaned poised over his erection. "This is for me." She opened her mouth and devoured his cock, gliding it as deep as she could. Then she drew back and sucked on him, the thick flesh filling her mouth.

"Oh, sweetheart, I want to make slow, sweet, passionate love to you and if you keep doing that, it'll all be over too soon."

"That's okay. We have all night." She licked him and twirled her tongue over the tip. "And I want to fit Connor in at some point, too." She grinned impishly. "Maybe at the same time."

Interest flared in his deep brown eyes.

"Now, when you say you'd like to *fit Connor in at the same time,* do you mean . . . ?" He purposely trailed off.

She stroked his cock as she arched her knee over his thigh so she was straddling him. "During our weekend together, we never had two of you making love to me at the same time. I mean . . . you know . . . one in front and one in back. I'd really like to try that."

The world spun around her as Travis rolled her onto her back. Then his cock brushed her slick opening and he glided in. She moaned at the exquisite sweetness of being stretched by his rock-solid cock.

He gazed down at her with a smile. "My God, if we had known that was something you wanted, we would have been doing it all weekend long."

"But then, there always would have been an odd man out." Thoughts of Erik cast a shadow on her mood.

Travis kissed her lightly. "Not tonight."

He drew back and glided deep into her again, sending thrilling heat through her.

"Tonight it's just the three of us, and Connor and I will ensure you are fully satisfied in any way you want."

She grasped his shoulders. "Well, good. Right now, I want you to *fully satisfy* me."

He laughed, then glided out and in again, filling her with his thick shaft. She clung to his shoulders as he pumped into her with powerful thrusts, speeding up as sublime pleasure swelled through her. She wrapped her legs around his waist.

"Oh, yes, that's so . . ." she gasped as he drove deeper still.

She moaned, swept away by blissful sensations trilling through her body. He groaned as he thrust faster. An orgasm blasted through her and he pinned her to the bed as he grunted his release.

Travis grinned at Connor's surprised expression.

"Really? Both of us?" Connor said.

"That's right."

Connor finished setting the cutlery in place beside the plates on the table. "Fuck, I wish we'd known she was into that on the weekend. Why didn't we ask her?"

"Because Erik didn't sense that as one of her fantasies."

"Yeah, but clearly it never hurts to ask."

Lindsay walked into the kitchen. "Mmm. Dinner smells delicious."

"And you look delicious."

She wore a small, black, lacy, sheer thing over a

satin-and-lace corset trimmed with red ribbons. It was cut high on the bottom, accentuating her long, sexy legs, and lifted her breasts up and out. They swelled over the top of the lace cups enticingly. She wore black stockings held up by the red-trimmed garters attached to the corset. The finishing touch was red shoes with impossibly high stiletto heels.

"Damn, woman." Connor's gaze glided up and down her sexy body. "You don't really expect us to eat with you dressed like that."

"Aren't you hungry?" she asked innocently.

Connor dragged her into his arms. "Fuck, yeah, but not for food."

Travis watched as he devoured her mouth. The heels gave Lindsay extra height, so Connor didn't have to hunch down to kiss her.

Travis walked behind her and slid his hands around and between their bodies to cup her breasts. Connor eased back and watched Travis stroking her breasts. Travis tugged at the lace and drew it down to bare one nipple. Connor swooped down and sucked it into his mouth. Travis pulled down the other cup and tweaked her exposed nipple.

Oh, God, it felt so good having both of them touch her like this. She'd wanted to look sexy for them, so she'd bought this special outfit. Clearly, they appreciated it.

Travis slid his arm around her waist and drew her back against his body as Connor licked and sucked her nipple. As Travis glided his other hand down her ribs, Connor switched to the other nipple. Sparks of pleasure flashed through her.

Connor wrapped his hands around her waist. "Let's put her on the counter."

Travis stepped away and Connor lifted her, setting her on the cold marble countertop by the fridge.

"What about dinner?" she asked with a grin.

"Fuck dinner." Connor switched off the oven, then turned back to her. "I've got what I'm hungry for right in front of me."

His mouth covered her nipple again, and Travis captured the other. She cupped each of their heads, stroking her fingers through their hair as they sucked on her.

"Oh, God, that feels so good."

Connor slid downward, then found the snaps holding the crotch of her corset and pulled them open. The strip of fabric fell away, baring her slick opening to him. He smiled, then lowered his mouth onto her. At his first lick, she gasped, then he plunged his tongue into her. Travis continued to suck her nipple, but his fingers found her opening and slid in beside Connor's tongue.

Connor licked her, then swirled his tongue over her clit as Travis plunged two more fingers into her.

Her head fell back against the cupboards. "Oh, yeah."

Travis sucked on her other nipple and she tucked her hand around his head, forking her fingers through his long hair. He thrust his fingers into her faster as Connor vibrated his tongue against her sensitive button.

She moaned as pleasure billowed through her, then exploded in a sudden, scintillating orgasm.

"Fuck, I want to taste her," Travis said, his eyes gleaming.

But instead of leaning down and licking her, he grabbed Connor's face and kissed him, deep and hard. Her heart drummed at the sexy sight. Travis eased back a bit, then his tongue glided around Connor's lips.

"I don't know about the two of you," Connor said once Travis released him, "but I'd really like to have a sandwich."

"Sandwich?" Lindsay's eyes widened at his sexy grin. "Oh, right."

Her stomach tightened, but that was just nerves. She wanted to feel both of these big, masculine men inside her at the same time.

"I've . . . uh . . . never done this before, so . . ."

Travis kissed her. "It's okay, sweet thing. We'll be gentle."

"I know."

Travis lifted her down from the counter, then led her into the living room to the back of the couch.

"When we're ready, just put your hands on there and lean forward."

She nodded, her stomach fluttering.

Connor shed his pants and boxers, revealing his swollen cock, and grabbed a tube of lube from a drawer in the side table, while Travis stripped off his clothes.

"Should I take off my outfit?" she asked.

"Hell, no." Connor pulled his shirt over his head and tossed it aside, then opened the tube.

"Does it matter who goes behind you?" Travis asked.

Her gaze went from one thick, hard cock to the other. "You're both so big, I don't think it matters."

Connor dribbled the gel onto his cock and rubbed it on until the whole thing glistened. He stepped behind her and kissed her neck. She leaned forward and grasped the back of the couch as Travis had suggested.

"Okay, doll, have you ever had anal sex before?"

"Yes. A couple of times."

"Okay, good."

She felt the tip of his cock press against her opening and she held her breath.

"I'm going to ease in really slowly."

She nodded and he pressed forward, his big cock-head stretching her. She pushed with her internal muscles to allow him entry. But he was so big. He eased forward slowly.

Finally, his cock-head was inside, gripped tightly by her passage.

"Fuck, you're so tight. You feel so good around me." Connor kissed her neck. "How are you doing?"

"Good." She felt so full with his cock-head in her ass, but she longed to have the rest of him glide inside. "Give me more."

He chuckled, then eased forward again, sliding deeper. Pleasurable sensations danced along her passage and she wanted to push back against him, but she stood still, letting him fill her at his own pace. Finally, she felt his groin against her butt.

"Oh, yeah, that feels so good." He tightened his hands around her wait. "Now I'm going to ease us around until I'm leaning against the couch and you're leaning against me."

"Okay."

He guided her around until she rested back against him. Travis stepped close and stroked her shoulder, then kissed her.

"I'm really looking forward to this, Lindsay," he said. "Making love to you at the same time as Connor."

She smiled. "Good. Then do it."

He pressed his marble-hard cock to her vagina and pressed forward. He glided in easily. Once his body was pressed against hers, he kissed her. Then he kissed Connor over her shoulder. She loved the feel of being sandwiched between their two big bodies, their hard cocks both inside her.

"Fuck, this is so hot I don't know how long I'll be able to hold on." Connor stroked her long hair to one side and nuzzled her neck.

Travis' fingers brushed her clit and she sucked in a breath. He nuzzled the other side of her neck as his finger cajoled her sensitive nub, blasting jagged, pleasurable sensations through her whole body.

"Ready?" he murmured against her ear.

"Oh, yeah."

Travis drew back, then glided into her again. His

hands grasped her hips and he held her to him as he drew back this time, which caused Connor's cock to drag along her back passage. Then Travis glided forward, pushing Connor's cock into her again.

Forward and back. Travis continued to fill her, while Connor's cock stroked her, too. She clung to Travis' shoulders as the double sensations quivered through her. Her heartbeat raced as the pleasure built. The hard cocks kept filling her again and again.

"Oh, God, this is so . . ." she moaned in pleasure. "Intense."

"Fuck, I'm going to . . . ahhh." Connor grunted and she felt hot liquid fill her.

Travis sped up, deepening his thrusts and she gasped.

"Yes . . ." she moaned as her insides trembled. "I'm so close." Pleasure swelled through her, then burst into sparks of pure bliss. She wailed at the intense sensations.

Travis groaned as liquid heat filled her again. He kept pumping and she rode the wave of pleasure higher and higher. She squeezed internal muscles and both men groaned.

Then she collapsed between them, her cheek resting against Travis' chest. She could hear his staccato heartbeat.

Travis stroked her hair while Connor nuzzled her neck.

It felt so good tucked between these two big men, all warm and cozy. She didn't ever want it to end.

———

Erik stepped out of the elevator into the penthouse. He wondered if Connor and Travis would still be up. The light was on in the entryway—the motion sensor would have triggered that when the elevator doors opened—but the living room beyond was dark.

He was tired and feeling glum.

In general, the evening had gone well, and as anticipated, Cheryl had invited him to join her and a friend after the party, but he'd bowed out. Although Cheryl was lovely and sexy and fun to be with, and her friend was any man's wet dream, he couldn't bring himself to participate. Ever since the weekend with Lindsay, all he could think about was her. He longed for her. Thoughts of having sex with any other woman just reminded him of Lindsay. He knew if he'd gone with Cheryl and her friend, the whole time he'd be imagining Lindsay—and that wasn't fair to them. When he was with a woman, he gave her—or in this case them—his full attention. Every woman deserved that.

She'd taken it in stride, but he was pretty sure he'd blown any chance of being with her again.

He raked his hand through his hair. Did he have special feelings for Lindsay or did Lindsay just represent every woman he'd ever lost?

He kicked off his shoes and put them into the closet. He just needed a little more time to put Lindsay behind him.

His gaze caught on a glint from the closet floor. A dark purple purse with a crystal heart attached to the zipper.

Lindsay's purse.

Eighteen

Erik's heart clenched. Damn it, what was Lindsay doing here? He'd specifically made it clear he didn't want to see her again.

But Travis had made it clear that they *did* want to see her again. And Connor knew that. No wonder Connor had pointed Cheryl in Erik's direction. He'd wanted to get rid of him for the night.

His gut clenched at the thought of seeing Lindsay again . . . and not touching her . . . not holding her. God, he wanted to feel her silky hair against his cheek again, her full lips against his, her soft breasts pressed tight to his chest.

God damn it, if he did see her right now, she'd probably be naked and moaning, enjoying the attention of Connor and Travis. Damn, his cock swelled, pushing against his pants. If he walked into the middle of that, he wouldn't be able to hold himself back.

But the living room was dark, so they were probably asleep. Or at least, in one of the bedrooms.

He walked into the living room and headed straight down the dark hall, dimly lit by the moonlight streaming in the living room windows, to his bedroom. He stripped down and climbed into bed. Just the thought of Lindsay in the next room made his cock ache. But he closed his eyes, refusing to think about it. Pushing aside thoughts of Connor and Travis lying close to her, her soft body against theirs, her breasts rising and falling with her breathing.

He sucked in a deep breath and then slowly released it, clearing his mind. Calming his body. Slow, deep breaths. In. Then out. Keeping his mind blank. His body limp and relaxed.

The darkness soothed him and he felt consciousness slip away.

At a moan from the next room, Erik jerked awake. A quick glance at the clock told him he'd fallen asleep for a short time.

"Oh, yes." Her soft words coiled through him, jerking his cock to attention.

"Fuck, yeah, doll. Your mouth feels so good."

He could imagine her mouth around Connor's cock. And probably Travis licking her slit. It would be hot and slick.

Lindsay's intense desire to have a man drive his cock into her had Erik bounding out of bed. He was at the door, his hand on the doorknob before he could stop himself.

Damn, his connection to her was stronger than he'd

ever felt. He leaned against the door, his cock aching. He wrapped his fingers around it and squeezed. It pulsed in his hand as he heard Connor groan in the next room. Then Lindsay moaned. Erik stroked his cock, longing to be inside her.

"Oh, God. Fuck me. I want to feel both your big cocks inside me again."

At her words, Erik clenched one fist against the door, while the other squeezed his cock tighter and stroked. Oh, God, had both men fucked her at the same time? Or did she just mean she'd sucked one of them while the other fucked her?

"I'll go in the back this time," Travis said.

Damn. They hadn't done that when she'd been here for the weekend. They'd thought it would be too much to ask of her and he hadn't sensed it as one of her desires. Maybe there was something to be said for just asking a woman.

Erik's heart ached that she had shared this with Travis and Connor and not him. Anxiety careened through him at the realization that the three of them were growing close without him.

"You okay, sweet thing?"

"God, yes. Now, Connor."

She gasped and Erik stroked his cock as he imagined driving into her himself.

"Oh, yeah. Faster."

Erik stroked faster at her words. Imagining driving deep into her heat.

He could hear her soft moans and the men's groans.

"I'm . . . oh, I'm . . ."

Erik's cock burst in release as she wailed loudly.

He slumped against the door, while the sounds of her continuing orgasm washed around him. Her sweet murmurs of pleasure. The men's groans as they released inside her.

He dragged himself from the door and toward the bed.

Damn, it was going to be a long night.

Lindsay yawned as she walked down the hall, tightening the sash on her robe. She wanted coffee. In fact, as she approached the kitchen, she could almost imagine she smelled fresh coffee. She went through the doorway and froze.

Erik stood at the counter, sipping from a mug.

Her heart ached at the sight of him. He was in his usual morning attire, just boxers, which left his big broad shoulders and well-sculpted chest naked. His hair was still wet, which meant he'd stepped out of the shower moments ago, since that short hair of his took no time to dry. He smelled of the woodsy musk soap he used, which made her want to lean in close and breathe him in. She longed to run her fingers through his hair and feel it brush along her skin, then to continue across his big shoulders and down his solid chest, then over his tight abs.

"Good morning." He glanced at her, his expression guarded.

"Morning." She walked to the cupboard and pulled out a mug, then filled it. "I thought you were . . . out."

He shrugged. "Plans changed."

She added sugar and cream to her coffee, then stirred. As the silence hung between them, her stomach tightened. Clearly, he was upset that she was here.

She took a sip of her coffee. The tension between them stretched taut.

"Did you sleep well?" she asked, desperate to break the awkward silence.

He put his coffee on the counter. "Not really. I had noisy neighbors."

Her cheeks flushed and her gaze darted to her coffee. He'd heard her with Connor and Travis. But she shouldn't be embarrassed. Not after the weekend of no-holds-barred sex they'd shared as a foursome.

Memories of him holding her in his arms, his big cock gliding into her, set her heartbeat racing.

Her gaze flicked back to him. "Well, you know the best way to deal with noisy neighbors. Join the party."

His gaze intensified as he watched her, his dark eyes glittering, then heat washed through her. Almost as if his desire thrummed through her, augmenting her own need.

"Would I have been welcome?"

Her heart thundered in her chest. Oh, God, of course he would have been welcome.

"With open arms."

His eyes darkened to the color of the midnight sky.

He walked toward her and tingles danced across her skin as his hands wrapped around her waist.

"Really?" He leaned in close and nuzzled the base of her neck, sending quivers through her. His fingers slid to the opening of her robe, his fingertips resting on the lapel. "Am I welcome now?"

"Yes," she murmured against his neck.

He captured her lips and his tongue slid inside her mouth as his fingers slipped under the fabric. Her nipple peaked as he glided closer. Then he stroked over the hard nub, sending quivers through her.

Erik couldn't believe he was touching her again. Her mouth so soft against his. Her nipple so hard. He squeezed it and breathed in her murmur of pleasure. He released her lips and pulled the robe back to bare her breast, then covered the hard nub with his mouth. The feel of the hard bead against his tongue delighted him. His cock swelled with need.

He shouldn't be doing this, but the swell of desire pulsing through her set his already rampaging need ablaze.

"Oh, God, I want you so badly." He licked her pebbled aureole.

Her fingers tangled at the belt of her robe, and she opened it, revealing her totally naked body. "Then take me."

He sucked in a breath to calm his erratic breathing. His hand glided down her naked body, stopping at her hip. He licked downward, then crouched in front of her. Her sweet pussy in front of his face. The soft blonde curls neatly trimmed. He leaned forward and pressed his tongue into her, the tip delving into her folds. He cupped her ass and pulled her forward, then drove his tongue in deeper. He felt the tight little button of her clit against the tip of his tongue. He licked and she moaned.

He backed her up and lifted her onto the counter. His hands slid over her hips, then to her pussy. He drew the flesh apart with his thumbs and stared at the little nub within the nest of folds. She whimpered as he stroked it with the tip of his finger, then he leaned in and licked it. She gasped, pulling his head tighter to her.

He slid two fingers inside her hot, slick warmth as he continued to flick her clit with his tongue. Her moans increased as he pushed his fingers deeper, then back, then deeper again. She tensed, and moaned a quiet release. Still he lapped at her, as moisture seeped from her opening.

His cock ached with the need to be inside her.

"Now fuck me, Erik. Please, I need you inside me."

His heart ached at her words. He shouldn't be doing this. He didn't want her needing him, any more than he wanted to need her. Especially with this intensity. But his cock throbbed insistently. He dropped his boxers and pressed his hard flesh against her slick opening, then pushed inside.

Fuck, she felt too damned good. Her hot, tight passage around him felt like heaven.

He drew back a little, then drove in hard, grinding against her.

"Oh, yes."

Her breathless words spurred him on. He thrust again and again. At her gasping breath, the feel of her soft breasts against his chest, and her hot passage massaging his throbbing cock, intense pleasure coiled through him.

"Oh, God, Lindsay, I've missed you."

"Me, too," she uttered between gasps.

She clung to his shoulders. God, he loved the feel of her fingers digging into his flesh.

He cupped her ass and lifted as she wrapped her legs around his waist. His cock drove even deeper into her sweetness.

She nuzzled his neck as he thrust, driving his need higher. Then she squeezed him inside. He groaned at the exquisite sensation.

She arched and moaned her release and the sound of it hurled him higher. Pleasure continued to bombard him until he exploded in pure, blissful ecstasy. He drove deeper and deeper as her moan turned to a loud wail.

Finally, she collapsed against him, her head flopping on his shoulder as she gasped for air.

"So, Erik. You're home."

Erik jerked his head around at Travis' voice. Shit, Travis stood at the door, an unreadable expression on his face.

Travis picked up Lindsay's robe and handed it to her. Erik lowered her from the counter and she pulled on the robe, hiding her naked, flushed body.

He locked gazes with Erik. "We need to talk."

Erik nodded. He pulled on his boxers and followed Travis.

Connor winked at Lindsay. "Don't go anywhere, doll. We'll be back."

Travis led Erik to Connor's room and Connor closed the door behind them.

Before Travis could open his mouth, Erik jumped in. "So are we going to start with why you invited Lindsay over here when you knew I didn't want her here?"

"You never said that," Connor said calmly. "You said you didn't want to see her again."

Erik turned to Connor. "If she's here, I'm going to see her."

"But you were supposed to be out," Connor continued, "so it shouldn't have been a problem."

"That's not the point."

"Then what is the point?" Travis demanded. "You said this was our place, too. Did you mean it, or are you going to dictate who we can and can't have here? Because that's not going to work for me."

Erik stared at him with narrowed eyes. "What difference does it make? It looks like you're choosing Lindsay over me, so I assume it won't be *us* much longer."

Travis' heart clenched. "It's true I want Lindsay to have a place in my life, but that doesn't mean I want to lose you."

"But if I don't want to be with Lindsay and you do, where does that leave us?" Erik swung his arm to gesture to Connor. "And where does it leave Connor?"

"I like Lindsay," Connor said with a smile.

Erik scowled and turned to Connor. "Sure, but aren't you afraid of her getting in the way of your relationship with Travis?"

"No," Connor said simply.

"Erik, I don't want to have to choose between you and Lindsay. And it doesn't have to be like that. What happened this morning proves that you want to be with her, too."

Erik snorted. "That was just sex."

Travis shook his head. "When are you going to admit that it's more than that with Lindsay? It's clear to all of us that the two of you have a real connection. If given a choice, she would choose you over us in a heartbeat."

Erik locked gazes with Travis, shock glimmering in his eyes. "Doesn't that bother you?"

"To be totally frank, you've always known that Connor would be my first choice. Does that bother *you*?"

Erik hesitated.

Damn, maybe he'd gone too far. Maybe Erik wasn't ready to hear that. But it was too late now. "You do know that, don't you?" Travis asked softly.

Erik drew in a deep breath. "Yes, I guess I did, but I still thought the three of us would make it work."

"That's just it. We can. I think the three of us are solid, and I think if Lindsay hooks up with you, we'll all share a great relationship." He locked gazes with Erik. "But it all depends on you."

Erik shook his head. "It won't work. What the three of us have is the most important thing to me. Bringing a woman in will just ruin things."

"You're just running scared. Because you've been hurt. Cyndi ripped out your heart, and every woman who left after her just augmented that pain, until you couldn't even trust yourself to know love when you saw it."

"And Becci caused you to doubt us," Connor said. "Even though we would never have dreamed of choosing her over you."

"But Lindsay's different." Erik stared straight at Travis. "Clearly, you would choose her over me. You've already done it."

"Fuck, Erik," Connor said. "That's not true. As much as Travis wants Lindsay, he wouldn't have agreed to her coming over if it weren't for me. I insisted, because I want him to be happy. We wanted to figure out if Lindsay would work with the two of us before we started working on you to accept her."

Erik's eyebrow rose. "And if I can't?"

"If you won't even try, then that means you don't care as much about us as you claim."

Erik stared at him, long and hard. Finally, he sighed. "I don't know what you want me to do. You know that she and I probably won't last. You're forgetting that women never stay once they find out what I can do."

"Lindsay's different," Travis said.

Erik frowned. "I thought every one of them was different. But I was wrong every time."

"There's one way to find out," Connor said. "Go tell her."

Nineteen

Lindsay's stomach fluttered as Erik closed the door behind them. Hope skittered through her that maybe he would give them a chance after all. He'd said he'd missed her, and their lovemaking had been so passionate, and his kisses so tender.

She turned to face him. At his tight expression, her heart sank.

"Look, Lindsay. It's obvious I have a strong attraction to you, and Travis and Connor would like to keep seeing you, but I still don't believe things will work between you and me."

"Why?"

His jaw clenched and he inhaled deeply. "There's something I haven't told you, and you're going to find it pretty strange."

She gazed into his blue eyes. "I'm listening."

"I have this . . . ability."

She frowned. She didn't know what she'd been expecting, but this wasn't it. "What kind of ability?"

"I can sense what women want. Sexually."

She smiled. "Yes, I like that about you."

"I don't just mean I know how to please a woman. I mean I can sense what you are imagining. It's like being empathic—I feel your desire—but it goes far beyond that. If you start getting turned on and you start fantasizing about, say, having sex with three men in an elevator, then I can actually experience that fantasy along with you."

"You're saying the reason you invited me for the fantasy weekend was because you sensed I wanted you when I first saw you on the elevator?"

He smiled. "I told you, you clearly wanted us."

"Yes, that's the point. You said you could tell. Because of the way I acted, not because you were in my head."

He sighed. "It doesn't really matter if you believe in my ability or not. You asked me to tell you why I don't think things will work between us and I'm trying to do that."

"Okay, so you have this ability. How does that affect us?"

"I've been in love before, and when I told her about my ability, she couldn't handle it."

She frowned. "So this woman left you because you knew how to please her?"

"No, at first she thought it was great, but after a while it started to freak her out. She said she didn't like me being inside her head. It made her feel too vulnerable. Like she had no secrets. She felt that it gave me some kind of control over her."

"So you're assuming I can't handle this ability either? Based on one woman's reaction?"

He shrugged. "It wasn't just one."

She understood that a woman might think if he could delve into the inner workings of her mind, whether by reading her thoughts, or emotions, then he would have a level of control. That she could hide nothing from him, and it would leave her completely exposed and vulnerable to him.

But she couldn't imagine Erik abusing his ability.

"So you think I'm like every other woman you've dated? And that's why you won't even give me a chance?"

He glanced at her. "You don't even believe me."

"It's not that I don't believe you. It's more that I don't fully understand."

"Okay. Let's say I give you a chance right now."

He surprised her by stepping toward her and drawing her into his arms, enveloping her in his warmth. He captured her mouth and his tongue dipped inside. His hands glided down her back, drawing her body tight to his, from shoulder to hip. Her breasts tingled with need as they crushed against his hard chest, only the thin silk of her robe between them. She could feel his sculpted abs against her stomach. When his hands cupped her butt, she could feel his swelling bulge.

"Now," he murmured against her ear, "imagine something that turns you on."

"I don't have to imagine," she said a little breathlessly.

He chuckled. "Just think about what you'd like me to do. Some kind of fantasy scenario would work best."

The poker game sprang to mind. Her stripping off her blouse as the three of them watched. Goose bumps skittered along her skin at the memory.

"Don't think of things we did during the weekend." He nuzzled her neck. "Like the poker game."

She stiffened at his accuracy, but of course it was just a coincidence. Memories of the ride in the elevator lurched forward, which was what he'd said had triggered the invitation.

"Or the elevator."

She drew back a little, but he didn't release her. "Okay, I was thinking about those things," she said, "but they are a little obvious. It doesn't prove anything."

"I know. That's why I said don't think of those." He nuzzled her neck. "Just let your mind go blank, then allow your inner desires to surface."

He kissed along her collarbone as his hand squeezed her ass and tremors rippled through her. His arm slid around her back as his other hand glided up her side, then around to cup her breast. His thumb found her nipple and thrilling sensations burst through her. He captured her lips and his tongue swirled inside, then undulated against hers.

The confident way his hands traveled over her body, the authoritative way his mouth mastered hers, took her breath away. She wanted him to own her. To push her against the wall and dominate her, confining her hands so she couldn't escape, while his tongue drove into her mouth, his hard, muscular body crushing her against the wall.

His arm tightened around her and she could feel his swollen cock pressing hard against her stomach. She felt the wall at her back before she even realized they were moving. His tongue drove deep, overwhelming her with his masculine presence. She drew in a deep breath, needing air. His big body pressed her tight to the wall. He captured her wrists and lifted them to the wall above her head. She arched against him, loving the feel of her breasts against his hard, muscular chest. Need overwhelmed her. He nuzzled her neck. Grasping both her wrists in one hand, he cupped her face in his other hand, his thumb stroking her neck as he drove his tongue deeper inside her.

Oh, God, she wanted him to fuck her hard against the wall. Right now.

His hand glided lower and he unfastened the sash of her robe; the whole time his tongue still invaded her mouth. His hand slid underneath and cupped her breast. Her hard nipple thrust into his palm. His hand roamed lower and she felt his fingers graze her stomach as he wrapped his hand around his big, hard cock. He tipped it down and flicked the robe out of the way, then glided his hard cock-head against her slick opening. Forward and back in an erotic caress.

She moaned and widened her legs, waiting for him to drive inside. *Wanting* him to drive inside.

He released her mouth, his tongue slipping from

inside her, and murmured against her ear, "Do you believe me now?"

Her eyelids popped open and she gazed at him with wide eyes.

"Oh, my God, you . . . you knew what I was thinking." A chill ran through her. And as much as she wanted that big cock of his to drive into her, she was unnerved.

His expression closed up and he drew back.

"And there we have it."

She nearly fell over as his big body moved away from her. Then he turned and strode from the room.

Twenty

Lindsay stared at the door Erik had just left. Her insides quivered and she felt woozy. He'd been inside her head. She walked to the bed on unsteady legs and slumped down on it, then pushed her hair back from her face.

Oh, God, Erik could read her mind? But no, he'd said that wasn't it. He'd said he could pick up whatever she was fantasizing about sexually.

A shiver ran through her. That was weird and overwhelming. A little scary actually, but why?

Lindsay stepped into the kitchen where Travis and Connor were preparing breakfast. Travis kept his attention on the bacon cooking on the griddle, but Connor walked to the coffeepot and poured a cup.

"So he told you," Connor said as he handed her a mug of coffee.

She nodded. "You both know about his . . . ability?"

Connor shrugged. "Yeah, of course."

She sat down at the table and sipped her coffee.

"I take it you have a problem with it." Travis eyed her as he put the plate of cooked bacon in the oven to keep it warm.

She gazed at him, and the disapproval in his eyes. He was judging her. Just like Erik had. Anger swelled through her.

"You know, Erik sprang this on me, then didn't even give me a chance to take it all in. He just up and stormed out, assuming I'm like every other woman who has left him over this."

"And you aren't?" Travis demanded.

She glared at him, her stomach coiling into a tight spiral. Her hands clenched into fists. It was clear neither he nor Erik believed there was anything special about her, or her connection with Erik. Fuming, she pushed herself to her feet, then turned and strode out.

Travis watched her go, his stomach twisted in a knot. He had wanted this to work out so badly. Had hoped that she would be the one to accept Erik. Just as she had accepted him.

"That was pretty harsh."

Travis glanced at Connor.

"You mean Lindsay not accepting Erik?" Travis asked.

"No, I mean you. Lindsay didn't say anything about

not accepting Erik. She was uncertain and shocked. What do you expect her to be when faced with something so bizarre? She needs time to get used to the idea. But you didn't give her that. You accused her of judging Erik, but . . . aren't you judging her?"

Travis scowled at his words.

"Man, I'm not trying to be mean. I'm just saying . . . doesn't Lindsay deserve better than that?"

That night, she tossed and turned in bed. She was hurt that Erik and Travis had assumed the worst of her. And at the same time, she felt guilty for reacting the way she had. But damn it, it had been a shock. She needed time to get used to the idea.

A lot of things made sense now. So many times she'd wondered at how he had been so in tune with her. How he had known exactly what she wanted. More than once it had felt like he could read her mind, but it had always been good. He'd made her fantasies come to life and that had been exciting.

She'd never heard of such a thing as this. Someone able to pick up someone else's fantasies. How was it even possible? And could other people do it? At that thought, she remembered some of the strange images that had wandered through her brain that weekend. Like when she'd thought about being with other women. Naked women. Those images almost seemed to come from outside herself.

A little chill ran through her and she wondered if Erik also had the ability to push images into her mind.

The next morning, as she sipped her coffee, a knock sounded at her door. She put down the newspaper she'd been reading and crossed the room, then peered out the peephole. Travis and Connor stood on the other side.

She opened the door.

"Lindsay, I'm sorry about yesterday," Travis said. "Can we come in and talk?"

She nodded, then stepped aside to let them in. "I've got a pot of coffee on."

She went into the kitchen and poured two mugs of coffee, added sugar to both and cream to Connor's, then brought them into the living room and set them on the coffee table. Connor sat in one of the armchairs opposite the couch and Travis stood by the window. Lindsay sat on the couch and sipped the coffee.

"It wasn't fair of me to assume what I did yesterday." Travis walked across the room and sat in the other arm-chair facing the couch. "It must have been a shock when Erik told you and I can understand your need for time to absorb everything. It's just that when Erik shot out of the penthouse right after your conversation . . ." He folded his hands together. "He's been hurt so badly before. I was just reacting to that. But I shouldn't have jumped to con-clusions."

She nodded. These men were so close and she under-stood Travis' protectiveness.

"I get it. When he told me . . ." She drew in a breath.

"When he proved it to me . . . It threw me off a little. Then he took off before I could say anything." Not that she would have known what to say. She was still dumbfounded and confused.

Travis leaned forward. "So the big question is, *are* you okay with it?"

She hesitated, uncertain of what to say. If she admitted she was still uncertain, then she'd be proving that she wasn't different from those other women. That she wasn't special.

"How can you not be okay with it?" Connor said in a light tone. "The guy knows what you're fantasizing about. He acts on that to make you happy. And that makes him happy. So the result is a couple of happy people." He grinned. "Or three, or four."

Travis leaned forward. "You don't really think Erik will try to control you, do you?"

Connor grinned. "Other than in a great domination scenario."

"Which you know he would stop immediately if you wanted him to," Travis added. "You do know that, right?"

She wrapped her arms around herself and nodded. "Of course I do."

"Then what are you struggling with?" Travis asked.

That was a good question. Her anger at Erik for storming out on her had waned. Just as she'd needed time to get used to the idea of his ability, she understood that he needed time to deal with his emotional issues around it. He'd been primed to believe the worst. Not because of her but because he'd been hurt before. It was a reflection of his own sense of self-worth, not a statement of what he thought of her. Thanks to Erik and the guys, her own sense of self-worth was higher than it had ever been, so she refused to let ego get in the way of what she and Erik could have if they could just get past these issues.

But she still had stuff to figure out.

"Well, I never knew such a thing was possible and I'm still trying to figure out what it all means." She pursed her lips and glanced from Connor to Travis. "Can he do this with you, too?"

"Yeah, it's great." Connor sipped his coffee. "You don't even have to tell him what you want. He just knows."

"And, can he . . . send you images, too?" she asked.

Travis tipped his head. "What do you mean, send images?"

"Sometimes I would get images of things that didn't seem like mine."

Connor shook his head. "It's a one-way thing. Erik picks up the other person's fantasies."

She rubbed her arms as another thought that had been tickling at her subconscious surfaced. "I wonder if . . . I mean, do you think it's possible that . . ." She stared straight at Travis. "I might have the same ability?"

Connor's eyebrows arched. "You think you can do it, too?"

Travis leaned back in his chair. "If you could, wouldn't you have known before now?"

"I definitely don't have it like Erik does, but when I'm with him I wonder if I sometimes pick up his desires."

"For example?" Travis prompted.

"Well, one of the times we were all out by the pool talking . . . I had this image of me with a couple of other women . . . I . . . and they . . . were naked."

Connor leaned forward with a glint in his eye. "And?"

"And, you know, we were . . . touching each other."

Connor grinned. "I definitely need more details so I can fully picture it."

Travis sent Connor a glance, then gazed back at her. "So you think that was a fantasy of Erik's, not yours?"

She nodded. "It makes sense. It didn't quite feel like mine." She sipped her coffee. "Now that I think back, there were other times, too. Where I'd have images of something really exciting but it seemed a little outside myself."

"If that's true," Travis said, "then you do have a deep connection with one another. I think we need to find out for sure."

The whole idea seemed unreal.

"How do you suggest we do that?" Lindsay asked.

Erik glanced up from his book. Connor and Travis stood in the doorway to his bedroom. He put the book down, hoping this wasn't about him and Lindsay. Travis had shown great restraint over the past week, not querying him about Lindsay or pushing him to call her, but Erik knew that wouldn't last. Travis thought Erik should try again with Lindsay, and Erik knew Travis would not give up on the idea.

"What's up?" he asked.

"We're kinda bored," said Connor.

"Okay."

Travis leaned against the door frame. "We thought we might do something together."

Erik glanced at the window, with the bright sunshine flowing in. "It's a nice day out. Want to go for a swim?"

Travis pushed himself from the door frame. "No. We were thinking more along the lines of digging out your handcuffs and . . . playing."

A slow grin spread across Erik's face. "Yeah, okay. You know where they are, right?"

Connor dug in his pocket and pulled out the handcuffs, and held them draped over his finger. "Way ahead of you, buddy."

Erik pushed himself from the bed and walked toward them, then reached for the handcuffs, but Connor pulled them away.

"No, this time, you're the one we want handcuffed."

Erik quirked his eyebrow. "Really? What if I refuse?"

Connor shrugged. "Then I guess we'll go do something else."

He turned to walk away and Erik chuckled, then grasped his shoulder.

"I didn't say I was going to refuse."

The feel of Connor's muscles rippling under his hand as he turned back sent Erik's hormones reeling. Soon they'd be stroking each other intimately, giving each other pleasure. His cock began to swell at the thought.

"Okay, then." Connor opened one cuff and Erik felt the cold bite of metal against his wrist as Connor snapped the bracelet on him.

Travis grabbed his arm and guided him to the wall across from the bed. There was a loop with a clip attached for just this kind of game, but usually it was Connor or Travis chained to the wall.

Travis grabbed the handcuff dangling from Erik's wrist. "Oh, wait. Take off your shirt first."

Erik tugged his shirt over his head and tossed it aside. Travis grabbed the empty bracelet again and snapped it around Erik's other wrist, then clipped the chain of the cuffs to the wall. Erik now stood with his hands fastened above his head.

Twenty-one

Lindsay waited in the hallway while Travis and Connor prepared the scene. Travis opened the door and gestured for her to come in. She peered inside and her breath caught at the sight of Erik chained to the wall, his big, broad chest naked. She wanted to stride over to him right now and run her hands over his solid muscles.

"So what's the fantasy?" Erik asked.

Connor chuckled. "Uh, real live cop handcuffed to the wall. What could be sexier than that?"

Lindsay totally agreed. Except if that cop broke free and grabbed her wrist, then threw her on the bed. Oh, God, had Erik picked up that image?

Erik's gaze darted to the door and he scowled as soon as he saw her.

"Why the hell did you bring her here?"

Her stomach fluttered as she stepped toward him.

"I wanted to tell you that I'm sorry about the way I

reacted when you told me about your talent," she said, "but I was just confused and shocked. I needed a little time to get used to the idea. But I did and I think it's great." She didn't want to tell him the rest yet. She and Travis and Connor had talked about it and they all agreed that she needed to prove it to him first, or he wouldn't believe it.

"So why am I chained up?" he asked.

"Well, that was our idea," Connor said. "We thought you might storm off if we just brought Lindsay in. We also thought that if you were turned on, you'd be more receptive to her presence."

"And you think that's a sound way for a relationship talk to go."

"No, you definitely need to talk. Afterward."

He raised an eyebrow. "Afterward?"

"Yeah, we want you to watch for a bit."

Connor drew her closer and his hand stroked along her shoulder. She shivered at the sharp bite of Erik's gaze, but he didn't protest as Connor unbuttoned her shirt, then slipped it from her shoulders. Goose bumps quivered along her flesh as Erik perused her breasts. Travis moved behind her and unfastened her bra, then Connor tugged it free.

Erik's smoldering gaze dropped to her naked breasts, and lingered. Her nipples spiked to attention. Travis stared at her swelling nipples, too.

"Erik," Travis said, still admiring her, "just look at her naked breasts. Her hard nipples."

Connor's hands cupped her breasts, his thumbs stroking her tight buds, and heat melted through her.

Travis walked to Erik and unzipped his jeans, then drew out his long, hard cock. "So what would you like to do to Lindsay right now?"

He stroked Erik's cock up and down, making Erik groan.

Lindsay had to stifle a whimper as Connor's mouth covered her hard nub.

Erik couldn't help it. He imagined leaning down and sucking her nipple, just as Connor was doing. Her small whimper sent his blood boiling.

As Travis stroked Erik's cock, driving his need higher, he imagined Lindsay drawing away from Connor and walking to the bed, then slipping off her shorts and undies and stretching out on the bed. He imagined watching as she slipped her fingers inside her pussy and stroked, her gaze locked on his raging cock, her tongue gliding around her lips as if she hungered for him.

The images careened through Lindsay in rapid-fire. They were coming too fast. She wouldn't remember them all.

She grasped Connor's head and lifted. Her nipple ached as his lips left it cold and wanting.

"I'm sensing what he wants," she whispered in his ear. "I think it's time."

Connor nodded and she walked to the bed, then slipped off her shorts and panties. She positioned herself, now totally naked, on the bed, leaning against the pillows as she'd seen in the images she assumed were coming from Erik and not her subconscious.

Travis squeezed Erik's cock and pumped it a few times, then let go. Erik's solid erection pointed straight at her. God, she longed to lunge for it and swallow it deep.

She stroked her breast, then glided down her belly to her mound. She cupped it, then slid her finger down farther and slipped into her velvety slickness. Erik's gaze followed her fingers. His cock twitched as she continued to stroke, her fingers lighting pleasure inside her, but she longed for Erik to stroke her. For his cock to drive inside her. Images drifted through her head of Erik breaking free of the cuffs and bounding toward her, then turning her over and smacking her bottom until it blazed red.

As disorienting as the images were, she realized he could do nothing while chained to the wall.

She arched her eyebrow. "Really, Erik? Corporal punishment?"

Confusion flickered in his eyes, then he gazed at her with renewed interest, though she could tell his hormones were affecting his thoughts as he continued to glance from her fingers to her face.

"That's right. I'd love to smack your bottom right now. Release me from the cuffs."

She shook her head, then drove her fingers inside again, enjoying the glow of pleasure rippling through her. "I don't think so. I'm more in the mood for pleasure right now rather than pain."

"Really?"

A wash of images flooded through her involving Connor and Travis.

She drew her finger from inside her and opened her arms. "Guys, I could use some help over here."

Erik watched as Travis and Connor sat down on the bed beside her and she guided Travis' head to her pussy. He could just imagine his own tongue gliding over her hot, wet opening as Travis licked her. She tucked her hand under her breast and lifted, urging Connor to take it in his mouth.

Erik's cock ached as his two friends licked and sucked on her delectable, naked body.

"Oh, please, Travis. Drive your tongue inside me." She arched against him and moaned. "Eat me until you make me come."

Connor sucked hard on her breast as Travis dove right into her pussy. Erik imagined her arching against him, moaning. Her pelvis arched against Travis.

He wanted to hear her beg Travis for more. To beg him to make her come.

"Travis, please . . . more!" She arched again. "Oh, God, please, make me come."

Travis guided her legs over his shoulders, opening them wider. He dove deeper and her moans increased.

Connor switched to her other breast and sucked. She wound her fingers in Travis' long hair and pulled him tighter against her. Then she wailed in release, her face contorted in ecstasy.

Erik's cock throbbed as Travis drew away, then stripped off his clothes and laid down beside her. Connor also stripped and stretched out on the other side of her. Both their cocks were fully erect, ready for action.

Erik longed to be there, lying so close to her. Touching her. Then climbing on top of her and driving inside her.

"He's awfully turned on." She smiled at Erik. "He wishes he were over here now, making love to me."

Was she trying to make him think she could read his fantasies? If so, she'd have to do better than that. Everything so far had been highly predictable.

She grasped both long, hard cocks beside her and began to stroke. "Since he can't fuck me right now, maybe one of you should do it for him."

"Or maybe both of us?"

She smiled at Erik. "What do you think, Erik? Both of them?"

Images skittered through him. Of Connor in front of her and Travis behind her. Of both of them driving into her until she screamed in ecstasy.

A big smile claimed her face and she murmured something to them. Travis grabbed some lube from the side table and coated his long cock with the gel. Connor drew her to her feet and she turned and bent over, leaning on the bed, as Travis stepped behind her. Erik's cock ached as he watched Travis press his glistening cock to her back opening. She drew in a deep breath as he pressed into her, then slowly eased forward.

"You okay?" Travis asked.

"Oh, yeah," she responded, her cheeks flushed in excitement.

Erik licked his lips as the big shaft continued into her. Once Travis was completely immersed, he held her against him and turned her around. He leaned against the bed as Connor stepped forward and positioned his cock against her pussy.

"You ready, doll?"

She nodded and he glided into her. She moaned at the deep invasion. Travis lifted her legs and she wrapped them around Connor's waist. Connor began to thrust into her. At the same time, Travis rocked his pelvis, pushing his cock in and out as Connor fucked her.

Erik's cock throbbed at the erotic sight in front of him, exactly as he imagined it.

"Oh, God, yes. Oh, yeah." Her words became thin and needy.

Connor thrust faster.

"Oh, yes. Oh—" Her fingers clutched tight around his shoulders as she moaned. "I'm going to . . . yes, deeper." She wailed. "I'm . . . ahhh . . . coming."

Her wail increased as she rode the wave of pleasure. Connor groaned and jerked against her. Travis began to moan, his thrusts making her gasp. Then he grunted his release.

Erik's cock ached, threatening to burst at any second. He could almost come just watching them. She wailed, clinging to Connor.

Finally, she collapsed between them, the three of them gasping for breath, their bodies glistening with sweat.

God damn it, he wanted to drive into any one of them right now. But preferably Lindsay.

A sweet smile claimed her lips as she gazed at him.

The mattress compressed under her as Connor tumbled her onto the bed, then rolled beside her. Travis glided up behind her and tucked his arm around her waist.

"Erik wants to come over here and fuck me." Lindsay turned and gazed at Travis' profile as he lay on the pillow next to her.

Travis smiled at her. "I'm not surprised."

"Or one of you."

"Still not surprising." Connor rolled onto his stomach, arching his ass up a little. His hand drifted down her stomach and rested on her mound. "I think we could all use a little nap."

Travis laughed, then rolled onto his stomach, too. He found her mound, also, and the two big, warm hands cupped her, one finger sliding into her slick opening just a little bit.

Both Travis and Connor faced her on the pillows and Connor winked at her, then closed his eyes. She allowed her eyes to drift closed, too. It was cozy and warm, and . . . arousing. Especially knowing Erik was watching them intently. She wanted to arch against their hands. Even though both the men holding her now had just driven into her until they all climaxed . . . she wanted Erik. She opened her eyes to see Erik gazing at her smugly, obviously sensing her desire for him.

She closed her eyes again and feigned sleep.

A powerful image washed through her, of Erik pulling himself free from the handcuffs and charging across the room, then driving his cock into her, deep and hard. *He trapped her hands above her head and thrust and thrust until she wailed beneath him. Pleasure pumped through her and she arched, her whole body stiffening as she achieved an exquisite release.*

She sucked in air as she opened her eyes and stared at him, still attached to the wall. She closed her eyes again . . . and was pulled into another fantasy . . . Erik kneeling on the bed between her legs, pressing her thighs wide. *He leaned forward and his tongue dipped into her.*

Her eyelids flicked open again. This was unnerving . . . but at the same time, totally thrilling.

An image of Erik pressing her to the wall, his fingers gliding into her slick opening, darted through her.

"Oh, God." She sat up. "Where's the key?" She climbed off the end of the bed, drawn inexorably to Erik. His big cock stood tall and proud and she wanted to wrap her hand around it, then her lips.

An image of his cock driving into her. She walked toward him and he smiled. She could just take what she wanted. He was the one chained to the wall. Why not tease him?

His long, hard cock sliding in and out. She groaned.

"Connor, where is the key?"

Connor pushed himself from the bed and walked toward the dresser, his flaccid cock swinging as he walked, and picked up the key, then strode to her side. She held out her hand, but he shook his head as he reached for Erik's wrists. "You'll never reach."

Given that Erik's hands were a foot above his head and Lindsay barely reached Erik's shoulder, he was right. As soon as Connor disengaged the cuffs from the wall and flicked open one bracelet, Erik moved like a blur and Lindsay found herself spun around, pushed back against the wall. Erik took her lips with passionate force, driving his tongue inside. Then his cock grazed her belly and—

"Oh, God."

His big, hard shaft drove into her, ramming her against the wall. He drove so deep she cried out in exquisite pleasure. His solid body held her firm as he grabbed her hands and pinned them above her head, the loose cuff still swinging from his wrist. She felt dominated and totally possessed.

He thrust again, then again, his lips moving on hers with mind-numbing authority.

Fuck me fuck me fuck me, she cried in her mind. He thrust and thrust and thrust. Pleasure stormed through her like a maelstrom. He pounded her against the wall and she wound her tongue around his as they both rode the wave of rising bliss. He released her mouth and she gasped, then moaned at the explosion of ecstasy.

As the joyful euphoria swept through her, she wanted his name on her tongue. "Oh . . . God . . . Erik." Was that her desire or his?

It didn't matter. As they joined in intimate bliss, she felt as one with him. Their bodies joined, their hearts beating together, their desires fused.

He released her wrists and lifted her knees, his cock still buried deep inside her. She wrapped her legs around him as he carried her to the bed. Travis slipped out of the way and joined Connor by the dresser as Erik laid her on the bed, his body above hers, his cock still inside her. And still hard. She gazed up at him and he eased back, his cock gliding along her passage in a gentle caress. He moved forward, then eased back again.

She grasped his shoulders and he leaned down and captured her lips in a gentle, coaxing kiss. She dipped her tongue between his lips as his pelvis moved forward, gliding his big cock deep again.

He released her lips and their gazes locked. The glow of his deep blue eyes warmed her. They stared into each other's eyes as his cock glided in and out. A deep ache grew within her. His cock caressed her, and she squeezed.

"God, I have missed you."

At his words, she moaned, pleasure of body and soul merging. She squeezed him and he groaned. His gentle thrusts increased. Faster. Deeper. She wrapped her legs around his waist, opening for him, allowing him deeper still.

"I've missed you, too."

The ache inside her intensified with his steady thrusts. He pulsed inside her, and she gasped as an explosion of pleasure caught her off guard. Then she catapulted to heaven, Erik groaning his own release. Silky heat filled her and she moaned again, then collapsed in his arms.

Erik held her tighter to his body, still reeling from the intensity of their lovemaking. He could feel the fast patter of her heart against his chest, echoing his own. It was as if their souls had merged with their bodies. Poignant and breathtaking.

And totally overwhelming. But he couldn't tear himself away.

She gazed up at him and smiled. "Erik, I love you."

Oh, God, was that her desire or his?

No, he didn't want to love her. He couldn't love her.

Suddenly, the memory of Cyndi walking out on him, suitcase in hand, flashed through his brain. All the pain of losing her came flooding back.

If he allowed himself to love Lindsay, he knew it would be so much worse if she left him. He didn't want to suffer like that.

She shifted beneath him and he eased to his side, realizing he was probably crushing her with the weight of his body. She gazed up at him uncertainly.

"Erik, I—"

He had to stop her words. "So you can sense my fantasies, too?" As unbelievable as it seemed, she had proven it. "Why didn't you tell me?"

"I really didn't know. I mean, until you told me you could do it, I figured the images were just my imagination. Or my own desire." She gazed at him and smiled. "It confused me when I started imagining myself with other women."

That image caused his cock to lurch, but he ignored it.

"So you haven't always been able to do it?"

She shook her head.

Lindsay had felt so close to him during their lovemaking. Almost as if they were one. But now, he was pulling away, and the distance between them yawned ominously before her.

And yet, seconds ago, she could swear he'd wanted her to say "I love you."

Or had that been her desire?

She drew up the covers and sat up. "Erik, I think we should talk about this. We seem to have a really special connection."

He drew away from her and sat up. "The connection is special for you, but I have it with everyone, remember?"

She sucked in a breath, feeling as if he'd slapped her. But what he said was true.

Was Erik the only man she would experience this with?

She was sure he was, because deep in her heart, she knew she loved him. And she longed to hear him tell her he loved her, too. She gazed at him and he scowled.

"Lindsay, don't make more of this than it is. The sex between us is hot, and we share an interesting connection, but that's it."

Oh, God, her heart clenched so tight she thought she'd collapse. Tears prickled at her eyes.

"You're right, Erik. It's nothing special." She hopped from the bed, clinging to the sheet, and gathered her clothes, then dashed for the bathroom. Once inside, she closed the door, then pulled on her clothes as quickly as she could.

When she opened the door, only Travis remained in the room.

"Lindsay, he'll come around. He just needs time."

She shook her head. "No. I'm done. He doesn't love me, and I don't believe he ever will."

She strode to the door. She was tired of rejection, and she was tired of trying to get other people to love her. Audrey. Glen. And now Erik.

She deserved better.

She marched out the door and down the hall.

Twenty-two

Erik stood at the edge of the deck staring over the city, his thoughts in turmoil. The patio door opened, then closed behind him.

"What the hell are you doing?" Connor leaned on the concrete railing beside Erik. "You can't tell me you're not in love with that woman."

Erik shrugged. "Okay." It wasn't an admission. He just didn't feel like arguing.

"So why the hell did you walk away?"

"Look, it's you and me and Travis. That's what's important to me."

"That's great. And we can still have that. With Lindsay."

"No. That just complicates things."

"Three guys in a committed relationship is already complicated . . . as far as other people are concerned anyway. But we don't care about any of that shit. We can make it work."

"But that's because you assume I'm in love with her."

"And you are. I figure the only problem here is that you're afraid she doesn't love you back. And even if she says she does, you won't trust it. You'll always be afraid that she'll leave. "

Erik just shrugged. Of course he was worried about that.

"But don't you wonder why you're comparing her to Cyndi and Becci when you know Lindsay is different? Of all the women in the world, you know she won't leave you because of your ability. Because she understands it."

Erik's heart thundered loudly in his chest. Fuck, why wouldn't Connor leave this alone?

"Erik, think about it. What is it that's really scaring you?"

He wanted to protest that he wasn't afraid, but Connor wouldn't buy it. And neither did Erik. As much as he wanted to convince himself he and Lindsay shouldn't be together, he knew that he wanted her in his life. Forever.

But with that thought, an ominous fear reared its head. What if they started a relationship, and he believed he had found his happily-ever-after . . . then she left? Not only would he be devastated because he'd lost the love of his life . . . he couldn't even blame her rejecting him on his ability. He couldn't point at his power and say, it's because of that. If Lindsay walked away . . .

She would be rejecting *him*.

Like his mother had.

What if he didn't measure up to what Lindsay wanted in a man? What if she left him despite everything they shared? Despite knowing each other's intimate desires and longings?

No two people could be better equipped to have a lasting relationship. So if she left him—if she rejected him—how would he ever recover?

"You know," Connor said as he stared at the city below, "every relationship is a risk. You just have to realize if she ever were to walk away, it's not your issue. If you've done everything you can to make it work—which you know you will—then if she leaves it's because something has changed in her."

Connor paused to let that sink in. "You know, we all know that you were profoundly affected by the women in your life. But it's also true that your father really did a number on you. The fact that he tried to force you to be another him instead of accepting the great person you are has made you doubt yourself at a very deep level. But, Erik, you are very easy to love."

Erik's heart clenched, unwilling to believe it.

"Travis and I know. We love you."

He stepped forward and placed his hand on Erik's shoulder. "You know, your father loved you, too."

"How can you possibly know that?"

Connor waved his arm to encompass their surroundings. "He left you all this. Wealth was his measure of success—what was most important to him—and he left it all to you."

Erik shrugged. "I'm his son."

"Sure, but he could have left it to his brother, or his business partner . . . hell, he could have left it to his dogs, but he didn't." Connor squeezed Erik's shoulder. "He left you his most precious legacy. His wealth. I think it was the only way he knew how to show you he loved you."

A well of emotion flared in Erik. Could it be true? Had his dad actually loved him? Erik would have settled for respect, but he and his father were very different people. Maybe that just wasn't possible. But the thought that his father actually loved him . . .

Connor pointed at the patio door. "And that woman in there loves you. I'm sure of it. So go in there and tell her how you feel."

Erik glanced into Connor's calm, hazel eyes.

Should he tell Lindsay he loved her? If he did, she might walk away. Hell, she might run, but . . . What if she didn't? What if she decided to stay and see where this relationship might go?

What if she chose to stay in his life forever?

His heart ached at the thought and he suddenly realized it was worth the potential pain to find out. He knew what that pain was like, and he'd survived it before. And even if she did reject him—and not his ability—he was strong enough to survive. Because the payoff . . . thoughts of her snuggled close to him in the middle of the night, her soft body pressed to him, her heartbeat synchronized to his . . . Oh, God, it was worth the risk.

He grasped Connor's arm and squeezed. "You're right."

He strode to the patio door and into the penthouse, and then toward the hall leading to the bedrooms.

"She's not here."

At Travis' voice, Erik turned around. Travis stepped from the kitchen, a steaming mug of coffee in his hand. "She left about five minutes ago."

Erik turned toward the entrance, determined to follow her.

Erik raced to the elevator and Connor and Travis followed along behind him.

"What are you two doing?" he asked.

"I'm going to drive." Travis jabbed the button indicating the parking level and the doors slid closed. "You'll race every light."

Connor crossed his arms and leaned against the wall. "And you won't?"

"Sure, but he's a cop and it looks bad if he's pulled over."

Erik glanced at Connor, who shrugged and said, "I want to know what happens."

Moments later, they were in the car driving up the ramp to the road.

"You know, Erik, Lindsay is pretty upset and hurt," Travis said.

Erik's stomach clenched. "I know."

"Have you thought about the fact," he continued, "that exactly the pain you sought to avoid—being dumped by someone you care about—is exactly what you've done to Lindsay?"

The words were like a jab to the stomach.

"Well, I'm glad you're on my side."

Travis gave him a quick glance. "I am. I just want you to understand that she might not be willing to jump back into your arms. Remember, she was treated like dirt by the last guy she dated. Clearly, he just dated her for the sex."

"Yeah, who wouldn't?"

Erik and Travis both stared at Connor in the rear-view mirror.

"I didn't mean *just* for the sex. I meant that sex with her is great and . . . Oh, fuck, never mind. You know what I meant."

"Anyway," Travis continued, "she met you and opened up to the possibility of a relationship and you pushed her away. When she found the two of you shared a deeper connection than anyone could ever imagine, you still turned her away. She's going to be extremely gun-shy."

"Thanks. You make me feel like total dirt."

Connor grabbed his shoulder and squeezed. "Then our job here is done."

"That's not my intent." Travis slowed the car, then turned right. "Connor and I encouraged her, even knowing you said you didn't want to see her again, so we all share in the blame." He glanced sideways and locked gazes with Erik briefly, and Erik could see the concern in his eyes. "I just want you to understand what you're getting into. And that Connor and I will do whatever we can to help."

"Yeah, man. We'd love to have her around all the time, so don't go using us as an excuse not to have her move in."

Move in? Erik's heart clenched but he realized not at fear of commitment, but at the deep desire to have her live with him all the time, to have the comfort of her in his bed every night. To share breakfast with her every day.

"Just get us there, Travis."

Travis smiled and nodded, then sped up as the up-coming light turned amber.

The light turned red and Lindsay stopped the car.

Oh, God, why had she allowed herself to believe that something could come of her relationship with Erik?

Relationship. It had never been that, really. He'd been clear from the beginning. It was a weekend fling. Fun with a stranger whose fantasies he'd sensed on an eleva-tor. A diversion, nothing more.

A honk sounded behind her and she realized the light had turned green. She accelerated.

But even when he'd told her outright that he didn't want to see her again, she'd persisted. And allowed her-self to believe. After all, she had this wonderful connec-tion with him, and an ability to read his desires. How could things not work out between them?

Because . . . he had that ability with everyone. There was nothing special about her.

She wasn't special.

He'd told her she was, but only to help her self-esteem.

She wasn't special to *him*. She was just another woman, like any other. He could read them all.

Nothing special.

Tears flowed again, blurring the road in front of her. She wiped them away, but instead of going straight on Garner Avenue, she turned right, heading for Jill's place.

"She's not here." Erik sat down in the passenger seat again. "At least, she's not answering her door or her cell phone."

"She probably doesn't want to talk to you," Connor said from the backseat.

Travis started the car and pulled out of the parking space. "Let's check the parking lot to see if her car's here."

Travis drove to the other side of the building and pulled to a stop. There was no sign of Lindsay's little red Tercel.

"Maybe she's at her friend's place. Jill." He'd lay odds that she'd want to talk to her close friend now.

Fifteen minutes later, they pulled into the apartment building Connor and Travis had moved out of a few weeks ago.

"There's her car." Connor pointed at the familiar red car in visitors' parking.

"You're saying he could actually read your fantasies?"

Lindsay glanced at Jill with tear-blurred eyes and nodded.

Jill sat beside her on the couch and hugged her. "Sorry, honey. As incredibly cool as that is, if he doesn't want to be with you, then he's just a jerk."

Lindsay shook her head. "No, he's not." Her previous boyfriend, he was a jerk, but not Erik.

Jill hugged her tighter. "Okay, he's not very smart then. You're amazing and wonderful, and if he can't see that, he doesn't deserve you."

Lindsay's heart ached. Jill's soothing words were meant to help, but they didn't. Erik just didn't love her and nothing could take away the sting of that rejection.

A knock sounded at the door. Jill ignored it and handed Lindsay a tissue. As Lindsay wiped her eyes, another knock sounded.

"Go ahead and get it. I'll be okay."

Jill nodded and strode to the door, then opened it.

"Hi, I'm looking for Lindsay."

Lindsay froze at the sound of Erik's voice.

"May I come in?"

Jill glanced toward Lindsay. Lindsay's heart pounded in her chest, but she nodded. As anxious as she was, she couldn't help wondering what Erik was picking up from Jill, whom Lindsay was sure was harboring wild and lusty thoughts about the tall sexy man in front of her.

But Erik only had eyes for Lindsay as he glanced past Jill to Lindsay's tearstained face. Jill stepped back as Erik strode into the room and toward her. He crouched in front of her, his midnight-blue eyes serious as he captured her gaze.

Hope rose, but she tamped it down. He was a decent guy and probably felt bad about hurting her. He probably wanted to make sure she was okay. But none of that changed the fact he didn't love her. And didn't want to be with her.

He took her hand as he searched her face.

She tugged her hand away and stood up. She didn't want him to look out for her. If it was over, it was over.

Erik's heart clenched, afraid he didn't have a chance in hell of winning her back.

"Lindsay, please listen to me. I was an idiot. And a coward. Rather than risking that you would eventually walk away, I drove you away first. The other women in my life . . . I could convince myself they walked away because of what I can do. But with you . . . If you walked away, that would mean you were rejecting me, and I didn't want to risk that."

She turned to face him and the pain in her glistening blue eyes tore at his heart. "So *you* rejected me."

His chest tightened. "I told you." His words came out low and tortured. "I was an idiot." He took her hands in his. "I'll do anything to make it up to you." He stroked a long blonde strand from her face and tucked it behind her ear. "Because I love you."

Twenty-three

Erik's heart skipped a beat as Lindsay stared at him in absolute disbelief. Then she turned her back on him and walked to the window. Jill hung in the background, watching hesitantly.

Erik realized his hands were shaking as he gazed at Lindsay's back. She'd walked away. Just as he'd feared.

And he had no one to blame but himself. The perfect woman had walked into his life and he'd driven her away.

He could either let her go and lick his wounds. Convince himself that what he had with Connor and Travis was enough, even though he now knew it wasn't. His life would never be complete without Lindsay.

Or he could fight for her. Convince her that he loved her, and that she loved him.

———

Lindsay stiffened as she felt Erik's hands on her shoulders.

"Lindsay, please. Look at me."

Slowly, she turned to face him. As soon as she gazed up at him, and saw the agony in his eyes, her heart clenched.

"I love you." His heartfelt words rang through her, quelling the numbness and stirring emotions deep inside.

His words were true. He loved her.

She blinked as her body started to tremble. Before she could utter a word, she was swept into his embrace, his lips capturing hers in a deep, passionate kiss.

She melted against him, her tongue colliding with his as she clung to his big, broad shoulders.

"I love you," he murmured against her lips.

Joy swept through her as she allowed herself to believe. A broad smile claimed her face and new tears sprang from her eyes. "I love you, too."

He laughed and kissed her again, then lifted her and twirled her around in a circle. Even when her feet rested on the ground again, she felt like she was floating on a cloud.

Erik loved her.

A knock sounded at the door and Jill walked over and stared out the peephole, then she opened the door with a smile.

"Connor and Travis. Welcome to the party."

"Hey, Jill." Connor stepped inside, followed by Travis. "So you two work things out?"

Travis smiled as he took in Lindsay's happy face.

Erik wrapped his arm around her waist and pulled her against his side. "We're good."

"So have you asked her to move in yet?"

Travis nudged Connor in the ribs. "Give the man a chance."

Move in?

"I just want to make sure he doesn't blow this," Connor responded.

Lindsay glanced at Erik.

"What do you say? Would you move in with me?" Erik smiled. "And Connor and Travis?"

"Wow." Jill sat down on the couch and watched in awe.

"I'll live with all three of you?" What did this mean for her and Erik?

"Yes, but you'll be living in my room." He kissed her hand. "I mean our room." He nudged his head toward his friends. "They just get to share."

She laughed. What more could a woman want? A man who loved her and wanted to spend his life with her . . . and his two best friends, and lovers.

"Honey, if you don't say yes, you're crazy." Jill smiled at Connor. "I wouldn't let an opportunity like this slip by."

Lindsay gazed into Erik's mesmerizing blue eyes, her heart bursting with joy. "Of course I will."

That joy mirrored in his eyes as he captured her lips and kissed her with a passion that took her breath away.

———

Elation rocked through Erik as he held the woman he loved in his arms. Her soft body close to his, as it would be every night in their bed. Close and warm. Sweet and comforting.

Her lips moved passionately under his and his flood of happiness shifted as he felt desire surging through her. She wanted him.

She nuzzled his neck and whispered in his ear, "Let's go home."

He grinned and took her hand and she followed him to the door. Jill grinned as she watched them go.

Connor and Travis followed them down the hall.

"I can't believe I'm being spirited away by three sexy men."

He could sense her awareness of Connor and Travis rising.

"It's like we're kidnapping you," Erik said.

Her eyes glittered. "It is."

Images of throwing her over his shoulder like a captive and dragging her into a room danced through his head. The three of them stripping away her clothes and tying her down. The images were so intense, his cock rose to full mast, straining painfully at his jeans.

"Hey, Travis, you still have a key to the old apartment?" he asked.

The person subletting the apartment didn't move in until the end of the month, which was next weekend.

"As a matter of fact, I do."

With that, Erik tossed Lindsay over his shoulder and

headed for the stairs. The old apartment was several flights down, but he didn't want to ruin the fantasy by waiting for an elevator. Lindsay giggled as she clung to his shirt. His hand held firm to her sexy thighs, and her delightful butt rested against his cheek as he hurried down the stairs. Travis went out the door first and raced ahead to the apartment. He had the door unlocked by the time Erik caught up, Connor right behind him. As Connor closed the door, Travis glanced at Erik for a cue. He knew when Erik was pursuing a woman's fantasy.

"Get something to tie up our pretty captive."

At Erik's words, a tremor of pure lust quaked through Lindsay. Erik strode toward the couch and flopped her down on it. Thankfully, it seemed the guys had sublet the apartment furnished. Their stuff didn't look like it would really fit in the penthouse.

Connor reappeared empty-handed. "No rope."

Of course, they must have packed everything but the furniture.

With a gleam in his eye, Erik slid his hand up her thigh until he reached the garter. She quivered as he flicked it open, then lifted her skirt to find the other and released that one, too. His fingers trailed along her foot as he unfastened her shoe, then tossed it aside. As he peeled off the stocking, Travis stripped off the other one. Her insides clenched in anticipation of what was to come.

Erik coiled one stocking around her wrist.

"Hey, if you tie her up first, we can't get her clothes off." Connor grinned. "At least, not without tearing them."

Big strong hands swooped down on her, unfastening the buttons on her blouse, tugging it from her shoulders, lifting her to stand. Her skirt slipped away, then she felt the hooks on her bra release. She sucked in air as it slipped away.

"No," she cried, realizing she was supposed to play the unwilling captive.

Erik glanced at her and she winked so he'd know she was playing along.

"Please let me go." She stood before them in only her panties and garter belt. Her nipples hardened under their intense scrutiny. Her garter belt slipped away.

"We're not going to let you go, doll," Connor said. "You're our prisoner and we intend to enjoy the situation to the fullest."

She sucked in air as he cupped her breast with his big, warm hand. Travis leaned down and licked her nipple, then took it in his hot mouth and sucked. She grasped his shoulders, as if to push him away, but she couldn't quell her soft moan.

"Are you going to tie her up?" Connor asked.

"Actually, I have an idea. Travis, get undressed and stand behind her."

Travis grinned. "My pleasure."

Connor took her wrists, as if she might try to bolt. She watched Travis pull off his clothes, anticipation building in her. The sight of his big, hard cock as he stripped off his boxers sent her heart fluttering. He stepped behind her and she felt his erection press against her butt.

Erik grasped her wrist. "Give me your wrist, Travis."

Travis complied and Erik wrapped their wrists together with the stocking.

"Stretch out your fingers."

Erik took her hand and pressed it to Travis', then wove the trailing end of the stocking in and out between their fingers, until her hand was matched tightly to his.

Travis curled his fingers, and hers moved with them. "Hey, this'll be fun."

Erik connected their other hands in the same manner and stepped back, smiling at his handiwork.

Connor stripped away his clothes. "Okay, I'm ready."

Travis moved his hand and cupped her breasts. Or, rather, she cupped her breasts, with his hands covering hers. He kneaded. Her hard nipples pressed into her palms. Her head fell back against his shoulder.

"You really must let me go."

"Yeah, that's not going to happen." Connor walked toward her, his big cock bouncing.

Erik grabbed a chair from the dining room and set it behind Travis. Travis flattened her hand on her stomach, steadying her, and sat down. Connor stepped squarely in front of them and Travis moved her hand to take hold of Connor's cock. Together, they stroked the big, hard erection.

"Yeah, man. Now in her mouth."

Staying in role, she shook her head, but her mouth watered at the sight of his big cock getting closer as Travis leaned forward, pressing her closer to Connor's cock. Connor wrapped his hand around her head as Travis pressed the cock to her mouth, then pushed it inside. Oh, God, it was so big. He glided it in and out and Travis tucked their other hands under Connor's balls, cradling them in her palm. He pressed up and squeezed her hand lightly around them.

"That is so fucking hot," Connor murmured.

Her glance flicked sideways to see Erik stripping off his clothes, too. Behind her, Travis' cock grew harder. Connor's cock glided deeper. In and out of her mouth. She started to suck. She couldn't help herself. It felt so good stretching her mouth.

He pulled out and Erik stepped in front of her. He pressed his big cock to her lips and it slid inside. At the same time, Connor pressed his cock to Travis' mouth and it disappeared inside. As the two cocks thrust in and out of their mouths, Travis found her breast. Their joined fingers stroked over her nipple, sending wild sensations thrumming through her.

She could tell Erik was close to coming, but he pulled out and stepped back. Connor tensed and grunted, releasing in Travis' mouth.

Erik grinned. "Travis, you should take advantage of your situation."

Travis moved their hands to cup her breasts again, then he used her fingers to caress her nipples. They hardened and ached. Then he guided one hand down her stomach, then under her panties. He dipped her finger between the damp folds, then inside.

"Hey, I want to see what's going on." Connor lurched forward, and tugged down the front of her panties. They slipped back up, so he grabbed the sides and tugged, then slipped them over her ass and down her thighs. Once they were off, he drew her knees apart and tucked them over Travis' knees. Travis pressed her finger back into her folds and stroked, then guided her finger inside again.

"Fuck, yeah." Connor's eyes gleamed with lust.

Erik's gaze also locked on her fingers. Images of his big cock gliding into her quivered through her mind, but she could sense he wanted to wait. She could almost feel the ache of his groin as anticipation grew in him.

Connor knelt in front of her and he stroked her wet folds, too, then pushed his finger inside. Now three fingers—hers, Travis', and Connor's—were inside her. She leaned back against Travis as delirious sensations thrummed through her.

"Ah, man, she is so wet." Connor leaned forward and she gasped as he licked her.

Travis chuckled. "I think our captive is coming around."

Connor laughed. "I definitely think she'll be coming."

"No, no," she murmured halfheartedly as Connor licked her clit.

"Don't worry, baby." Connor grinned up at her. "I won't stop." Then he returned to licking her.

Erik stepped closer and pressed his cock to Travis' mouth as he watched Connor licking and sucking her. As his cock glided between Travis' lips, she lifted her head and licked his balls.

"Oh, yeah." His eyes closed and he moaned as she licked, then opened her mouth and drew one shaven sack into her mouth. "Oh, fuck, yeah."

Connor pushed hers and Travis' fingers out of the way and pushed two fingers into her as he sucked her clit. The big fingers fucked her like a small cock, in and out, as his tongue worked magic on her clit, sending pleasure soaring through her. She licked Erik's balls, then released them on a long moan as an orgasm swept through her.

She sucked in air, catching her breath after the delightful pleasure, but knowing it could be so much more.

"I want you to fuck me. All of you. At the same time." She didn't know exactly how that would happen, but she wanted it. And she wanted it now. "Please fuck me."

"She's a bossy little captive." Erik winked.

He pulled her and Travis to their feet and pulled the bindings from their hands. Travis wrapped his hands around her waist and hurried her to the back of the couch and leaned her over. Connor grabbed a bottle of lube from the bathroom and tossed it to Travis.

A moment later, Travis' hard cock pressed against her back opening and slowly pushed inside. It was big and hard, and stretched her delightfully.

"Oh, God, yes."

Once he was fully inside her, he pulled her against him.

"Now, you said all of us, eh? Are you sure?" Erik grinned, his cock shiny with lube.

Connor tossed the bottle onto the coffee table, his cock also glistening with the stuff.

She nodded, not entirely sure she knew what they had in mind. She had assumed one would be in her mouth, but they wouldn't have put lube on for that.

Travis turned her around, still inside her, and leaned back against the couch. Both Erik and Connor stepped in front of her. Erik pressed his cock to her opening and glided in. She groaned at the exquisite pleasure of his big cock pushing into her. Then he drew out and Connor slid inside. She assumed they would take turns, but Erik pressed his cock to her opening while Connor was still inside. Impossibly, she watched Erik push into her right alongside Connor.

"Oh, God, you're both too big to do that."

Erik chuckled. "I'm glad you're impressed with our size, but honey, I think we can do it."

Slowly, and patiently, he eased forward. She felt stretched wide, but the excitement of what was happening held her mesmerized. He eased in a little at a time. Finally, he was fully inside. Both of them, their hips pressed tightly together, stood with their big cocks inside her.

All three men were inside her. Her vagina clenched and she moaned at the resulting wash of pleasure. "I can't believe you're all inside me."

"No kidding. It's fucking hot." Connor tilted his pelvis a little, pressing his cock a little deeper. Quivers tingled through her. "I might just come on the spot."

Erik pressed a little deeper into her and she clenched around them. She trembled at the intense sensations buffeting her insides.

"Oh, God." She clenched around them as pleasure swelled through her. She moaned and Erik and Connor drew back a little, then glided inside.

They moved in and out, just a little, stretching her. The pleasure pulsed, then surrounded her in a cocoon of wild sensations. Cocks moved inside her. Front and back. In and out. She moaned as her pleasure catapulted to a new level. Her nerve endings tingled as heat blazed through her, propelling her to pure ecstasy. She wailed as she blasted to heaven.

Several moments passed as she stood slumped against Travis, still sandwiched between them.

"That was . . . incredible."

Erik leaned in and kissed her. "And there'll be plenty more incredible experiences from now on."

Erik and Connor drew back, their cocks slipping from inside her. Erik took her hand as she stepped away from Travis' support.

"So we might be a foursome now," Travis said, "but I think Erik and Lindsay could use a little alone time."

Erik grinned and pulled Lindsay with him toward the hallway. "I'm glad you guys understand."

He guided her to a door at the end of the hall and

stepped inside. It was a big bedroom with a king-sized bed. He closed the door behind them and then swept her into his arms and kissed her. She melted against him, love swelling through her. Their tongues danced together as he guided her to the bed.

God, this was really happening. She was in a relationship with three men, but one she was truly in love with. She found herself lying on the bed with Erik on top of her, his tongue still gliding inside her.

"My God, I love you so much." He smiled at her, then leaned in and lapped at her breast. Her nipple swelled in his mouth. He sucked and she moaned in pleasure. His hand glided down her stomach and he found her wet opening. His fingers stroked inside her and she longed for his big cock to enter her again, even though he'd been inside her only moments before.

This time would be different. Just between the two of them. Intimate. Passionate.

Knowing he loved her.

He smiled and she felt his cock-head glide down her stomach, then press against her opening. She tingled in anticipation as he eased inside, gliding deeper. Moving slowly. Then he was fully immersed. She wrapped her arms around him, holding him close, loving the feel of his cock deep inside her.

They stayed like that for several moments, neither of them moving. His heartbeat close to hers. Thumping in unison. The rise and fall of his chest in time with her breathing.

"I love you, Erik."

He smiled. "And I love you."

He drew back, then glided deep again. She tightened around him. As he pulled back again, the ridge of his cock-head massaged her passage. Then he drove deep again.

"Oh, that feels so good," she murmured.

He chuckled and thrust again. "And you feel good around me."

His big, hard cock moved inside her. Stroking. Driving her pleasure higher. Until it swelled out of control. She moaned as he thrust faster and faster. She cried out as passion and pleasure collided in an explosion of ecstasy. Rapture blossomed within her and she clung to him as they both plummeted to the edge of forever, joy quivering through them.

Finally, he rolled to her side and drew her against his body.

Giddy with delight, she laughed. "I am the luckiest woman in the world. Not only do I have an incredible man who loves me, but he comes with two spares."

He laughed and kissed down her torso, then rested his head on her belly, a content smile on his face.

At the sound of groans from the next room, he laughed. "And the great thing is they're quite capable of amusing themselves when we want to be alone."

She smiled. "Life couldn't be more perfect."

Fulfill all your wildest fantasies with Opal Carew...

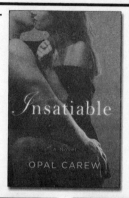

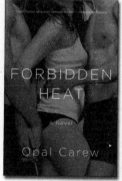

"Beautiful erotic romance...real and powerful."

—*RT Book Reviews*

 St. Martin's Griffin